SOMEWHERE ALONG THE WAY

BY

WAYNE FOX

FORWARD

This book is fiction. It is set in the days after WWII ended. It is the story of a US Navy pilot who went to the aid of a country off the coast of Venezuela. The country is also fictitious. The fact that German war criminals did seek refuge in South American countries is actual. It is also true that some took the spoils of war, such as gold and other valuable items with them. I am not suggesting that Venezuela was instrumental in this. It likely took place in many countries, and Venezuela may not have even harbored such people. As mentioned before, it is fiction.

My religious faith is real; the story is not.

DEDICATION

This book is dedicated to the men and women I had the privilege of serving with in the Navy. Those who gave their lives have a special remembrance. There were all too many.

It is also dedicated to my family for their love and unending support.

Cover designed by Wayne Fox

This book is a work of fiction. Names, characters, places, and incidents either are products of the author's imagination or are used fictitiously. Any resemblance to actual persons, living or dead, events, or locales is entirely coincidental.

Wayne Fox
navytailhook1@gmail.com

Printed in the United States of America

First Printing: May 2020
Name of Company

ISBN-9798639307676

CONTENTS

Lt. Wayne Fox in 1959

CHAPTER I

I felt someone shake me and whisper my name. I fought reality and tried to return to sleep, but the shaking resumed, and I heard my name again. This time a little louder and with more authority. "Bob, wake up, I need to talk to you, this is Fred."

I managed to open my eyes and saw a German officer standing over me with an extremely excited expression on his face. "What's wrong, Fred. You look like you saw a ghost."

"Worse than that, Bob. We just got word that the Russians are only a few miles away and will be here in a few hours. The entire camp is awake and trying to get ready. There is talk of shooting the prisoners. Some SS troops are trying to make it here to help, but I am not sure they can get here in time. If they do get here ahead of the Russians, I am sure they will shoot all the prisoners. I have to get you out of here."

"I can't leave my men, Fred. Can you talk the Commandant into turning all the prisoners loose before the SS gets here?"

"I don't know, Bob, it's pretty hectic right now."

"Fred, can you get me in to see him, maybe I can convince him?"

"We can try, Bob. The Commandant is a God-fearing man. I don't know if he will talk to you right now, he has a lot going on."

"We have to get through to him. I think I have a chance to convince him if I can talk to him. Fred, whatever happens, I want you to know we are friends. You are the reason I am still alive. What happens now is out of your control."

"Thanks, Bob. I haven't given up yet. Let's go."

Fred and I left the prisoner's barracks and started for the Commandant's office. The entire camp was in a state of confusion, a kind of controlled chaos. When we entered the Commandant's office, he looked up and said to Fred. "I am busy, Captain, what do you want."

"Sir, Lieutenant Baker would like to have a word with you."

"Make it quick, Lieutenant; I will give you two minutes."

"Sir, the SS is on its way here. I feel they will shoot all the prisoners. If they do, I think the Russians will shoot all of you when they get here. I think you know they are ruthless."

"I am very much aware of how the Russians operate. The Commandant looked at Fred. "Captain Wilhelm, take six guards and move the prisoners to the rear. Move as fast as you can so the Russians don't catch you."

Fred came to attention, clicked his heels, saluted, and said, "Yes, Sir."

Fred and I started back to the prisoner's barracks. "Get everyone going, Bob. I'll get six men and be right back."

"I'll have everyone ready, Fred."

As I walked into the barracks, I was deluged with questions. It was apparent that something big was going down, and everyone wanted to know right now.

I raised my hand, asking for silence. "The Russians will be here in a few hours, but the SS will get here first. You all know what that means. If you want to stay alive, get what you can in five minutes, and be ready to travel. Captain Wilhelm will be in charge, so we know he will take care of us if he can. We will have to carry those that can't walk.

I think we were ready in under five minutes. There were thirty-six of us, with four unable to walk. When Fred arrived, he had a vehicle that could carry the wounded. We started in a very jubilant frame of mind. We had only made about ten miles when we ran into a roadblock. Some of the Russians had circled to attack the camp from the rear.

At first, the Russians appeared to be taking us prisoner, along with the German guards. I finally convinced them we were on their side.

The German soldiers were marched to the side of the road and lined up. It became apparent that they were going to shoot them, so I quickly stood between the German and Russian soldiers. The Russian officer very adamantly motioned for me to get out of the way. Still, I stood firm and yelled at my men to see if anyone could speak Russian.

One man came forward and told me he was able to speak Russian well enough to talk to the officer.

I told him to tell the Russian officer that these men were trying to help us. I was not sure about all of them, but I sure didn't want Fred shot.

The conversation between my interpreter and the Russian officer did not appear to be going very well. The Russian was shouting and waving his arms. Finally, my man turned to me. This guy says they are enemy soldiers, and they will be shot.

I wasn't sure what to do, so I just walked over and stood in front of Fred. I turned to my man and told him to tell the Russian officer that this man saved my life, and I would not allow this man to be shot.

After more shouting and arm-waving, the Russian officer said he would allow him to live, but the others would be shot.

I wasn't sure what to do until I again noticed the Russian officer's rank. I was not sure of what rank he held, but I had to do something. I told my man to tell him that I held a higher rank than he did, so he would have to obey me.

The Russian officer had a very puzzled look on his face as he scrutinized my officer's bars. I knew I had him on the ropes, so I just told Fred to have his men fall in with mine and for him to join me. As Fred walked over to where I was standing, The Russian officer just stared at me. He finally said something in Russian. I was told that he said that I would be responsible for the Germans, but he would not give up his command. I gave him an even stronger stare and shook my head yes. He turned around and walked away.

As he was leaving, he started shouting orders to his men. I was told he was ordering them to get ready to move out. We could now hear gunfire coming from the direction of the prison camp. We assumed the Russians had started their assault. I don't think the German SS troops had time to get there, so we knew the guards at the camp were taking a lot of punishment.

We continued to move away from the prison camp, making an effort to get as much distance between us as possible. We knew that we had both German and Allied troops in the area. It became a guessing game as to whether we would meet which one first. Fred told me the end had to be near. He had heard rumors that Hitler was dead, but he was not sure. The prison camp we were in held many newly captured prisoners. I had been there about seven months after being shot down. I was one of the prisoners that had been there the longest. Fred and I had immediately formed a strong friendship with him, trying to look out for me. When they could not get rid of the prisoners fast enough, some were shot to make room for more. Fred had pulled me out of that line more than once. I owed him my life, and I did not intend to ignore what he had done.

Fred agreed with me that Germany would lose the war, so we would try to contact Allied forces if at all possible. I, in turn, told Fred I would see that the German soldiers would be treated as well as I could manage.

We struggled on for five more days, trying to forage for food when and where we could. Somehow, we managed to keep going. We did lose three of the prisoners toward the end when it was tough going, and supplies were nonexistent. We took the time to bury them and continued.

On the sixth day, we were on a lonely deserted road in France. I was not sure just where we were. We had just rounded a bend with Fred and me in front of the group. I heard shots ring out. I yelled for white flags to be waved and tried to locate the shooters.

"Fred, do you see anyone? I did not receive an answer, so I whipped my head around to Fred's direction. Fred was on his knees, looking at me with a terrified look on his face. He reached out for me and grabbed my arm. I tried to catch him, but he took me down with him. We fell to the ground together. I was in disbelief as a trickle of blood found its way from the corner of his mouth and reddened my arm. I knew he was dying, but I held him in my arms and felt the warmth of his blood on my chest as he died. I lowered him to the ground, still holding him, not ready to accept what just happened.

I rose to an upright position, ready to seek vengeance on whoever did this. I saw before me a young girl. She just said, "I didn't know." And allowed tears to dampen her cheeks ever so slowly.

I said, "I know," and added my tears to hers.

We had lost Fred and two other German guards. The attackers were the Free French; they had seen our group with seven German soldiers, and we prisoners. They could only accept what they thought they saw, and that was German soldiers with weapons escorting prisoners.

I slowly drew the young girl to me, hugged her, and said, "You did what you thought was right. You had no way of knowing. Neither God nor I will condemn you. Go in peace and leave the memories of war on this battlefield, try to accept, and forget what happened here today.

The Free French took us with them to their town and took care of us. They told us that the Germans had pulled out, but were still active nearby. They vowed to continue their resistance till all were gone. They did not know, at the time, that the Germans with us were trying to help us since they were sure the war would soon end.

I was told the young girl, that shot Fred, was only seventeen years old. She had been active in the resistance since she was fifteen. I wondered how a young person like her could ever live a normal life again. It was sure to be more difficult now.

It took us another month to get back to the states. We were transferred from one underground system to another. My ship that I was attached to was still in the Mediterranean Sea. My squadron had been temporarily assigned to a Marine base so we could give the Marines some help. They had lost several pilots and needed our support.

We met many brave people who had their lives on the line almost daily. It was an honor for me, I know.

By the time we arrived back in the States, the war in Europe had ended. The Japanese were still holding on. It was thought they would fight to the death. It was felt that the invasion of Japan would cost a million lives.

We knew we would all get some leave before we had to join our forces in the Pacific. None of the Navy people were anxious to fight the Japanese again. We knew from experience the Japanese were ready to die for their

Emperor and wanted to take a lot of Americans with them. We will try to forget that for a while and enjoy our time at home.

It was good to be back home again. Mom, Dad, and my sister heard at first that I had been killed in action, but later learned that I was a prisoner of war. There were many voids among my friends, and many still in the service.

I had seen a lot of action in the five years I had spent in the Navy. After receiving my wings and commission as an officer, I had been on two war cruises. Both as a carrier-based fighter pilot. I had seven enemy aircraft to my credit. Five Japanese and two German planes. I was shot down once in the South Pacific and again in France. The first I had to bail out over water and spent several hours in a one-man raft before I was picked up. The second I went down in my Hellcat and was captured by the Germans. I was injured in the last, but not too severely. I was reported as missing in action, but it was changed to killed in action later. Sometime after that, the Red Cross made contact with me while I was in a German prison camp and notified my family that I was still alive.

I was given thirty days' leave since I had been a prisoner of war, very welcome at the time, but it soon became tiresome. Most of my friends were in some form of the military, and some would never come home. There were still some of the girls around; however, many had joined some type of military unit, and many were away working at a war plant. The girl I had dated while I was in school had joined the Army and was stationed in California.

I had a few friends to spend some time with. Some could not pass the physical for military service, some were home on leave, and some had been discharged due to injuries received.

The time was passing slowly, and I was beginning to get a little restless. I wanted to get back to my squadron and find out more about what had taken place. They had been relieved of duty in Europe and were heading for the South Pacific to help fight the Japanese. I was anxious to know who was missing from our ranks and everything that had happened in the time I was gone.

Toward the end of my leave, I was notified that their carrier had been in a Typhoon and had received damages. They were being redirected to Norfolk for repairs. I was told I was to join them there.

I became more anxious as the time drew near to return to my ship. I had my train tickets purchased several days in advance, and my bags packed. It was a tearful time when I boarded my train for the East coast. I assured my parents that I would come home in one piece. I hoped that the promise would hold up. I was starting to wonder if that would prove to be true.

After I debarked from the train, I was directed to a military bus that was a shuttle to the base. The bus was packed with sailors who would be returning from leave and reporting back in for duty. At the base, I checked in with the duty officer and was informed my squadron was being moved back to Alameda in California. All had left the day before. I would now have to catch a plane to the West coast to join them. I was in disbelief. I had just traveled from Iowa to Virginia, and now I was to go back the way I came and go to California.

I was able to catch a Navy plane that was going that way, so I hitched a ride with them. Two days later, I set foot at NAS Alameda in California. I think half the squadron was there to greet me. It had been over nine months since I had seen them. We had a lot of catching up to do and lots of stories to tell. The squadron had lost four pilots after I was captured, and had four more wounded. They had seen a lot of action in those months. There were also a lot of new faces among the old ones. It was a good and bad time. Good to see all my old friends and bad for all my friends who would forever be absent. Like always, a lost friend is only mentioned briefly but remembered always.

There would be a lot of changes made. Many of the pilots would be assigned to other squadrons and shore duty, while many new faces would be among those who stayed. No one knew what to expect in where he would go or if he would stay. We knew that we had several weeks before all this took place. We were just going to enjoy our time here and not think about the future,

Our attitude was to live for the moment and not think about the future. As long as the Officer's Club did not run out of beer and whiskey, and if we could find a young lady to dance with on occasion, we would be happy. New airplanes would be coming into the squadron so we would get our flight time in and earn our flight pay. Some may be leaving sooner than others, and some may stay. I don't think anyone gave it much thought. We will just set back and take one day at a time.

Finally, some of the new planes came in. They were the newer F4U Corsair. We had been flying the F6F Hellcat and were excited to fly this bird. It kind of did look like a bird with its gull wings. Someone nicknamed the craft, 'Hognose,' a very fitting nickname given its extremely long nose and a large four-bladed prop. We all wanted to fly it first, especially if we thought we would be transferred to some other duty station.

This particular morning, Stan and I strolled down to our ready room in our hanger and flight area. Stan was my close friend who had bunked with me almost the entire time we had been in the Navy. I had a note in my notice box that the Skipper wanted to see me. I assumed it would be some sort of orders or information as to where my new duty station would be. I secretly was hoping Stan, and I would get the same duty station. When I arrived at the Skippers office, I knocked and was told to come in. I was right about the assumption about my orders. I would report to NAS Jacksonville and be assigned to Fighter Squadron VF-21. The Skipper congratulated me and shook my hand. He told me that he had heard that VF-21 was to get a new airplane. We would be the first squadron to fly these planes. They were the F8F Bearcat. He continued, "I have not heard much about the F8, only that it is rumored to be something very new and very different. That is about all I know about it."

"Thanks, Skipper, did it say when I was to report to VF-21?"

"You will leave here in ten days and be given three days to get there. You will train for a few months to get to know everyone and establish who flies with who."

"Did Stan get his orders yet; I am hoping we will be together in our next duty station?"

"They just came in. When you go back to the ready room, tell him to come down to my office. I'll let him tell you where he is going. Good luck at your new duty station. I am sure you will be a major asset to them."

"Thanks, Skipper, I'll tell Stan to report to you." With that, I left the Skipper's office and started for the ready room. I found Stan with a cup of coffee and reading a Navy publication. I told him his orders were in and to report to the Skipper.

"Did the Skipper tell you where I was going? By the way, where are you headed to?"

"I'm going to VF-21 in Florida. The Skipper said he would let you tell me where you are going. Let me know what you find out."

"Will do, kind of anxious to find out." With that, Stan headed for the Skipper's office.

I grabbed a seat in the ready room, kicked back, and tried to relax. I was sure I would get to fly the Corsair a few times yet, but I was also curious about the F8. I had not heard anything about the plane and was anxious to get in it and fly it. It did not seem like a long time before Stan was back.

"Well, Stan, is it good or bad news?"

"That depends on how you look at it. The good news is that I am going to a fighter squadron." Stan stopped and looked at me with a big grin on his face.

"Come on, what is the bad news?

"The bad news is that it is VF-21."

"Stan, you mean I have to bunk with you again?"

"No, Bob, you get to bunk with me again. If that will be too much of a hardship, I can find someone else."

"I guess I can put up with you again. We can travel together and maybe stop at my home in Iowa and yours in Alabama. They should be pretty much on the way."

"Bob, you and I were just home not long ago. I know you had some leave when you got back to the states. I took some when I got home, and our ship was in Norfolk, but I think it would be nice to stop at both our places."

"Sounds good to me, Stan, I'm anxious to see this F8, the Skipper made it sound interesting."

The next few days seem to go slower than usual, but we were getting set to make our trip, although we didn't know what problems we would have when arranging our transportation. Getting gas would be a problem. That would be a bit complicated, and neither one of us has a car. We could go by train, but that would not be easy either. I think passenger space was at a premium. We might have priority, but that is not worth anything if space does not exist.

"Bob, I think the only thing left for us is to try to tag on to a Navy plane heading in that direction. Maybe the Skipper has some pull and can get us on something heading to Florida."

"Let's go talk to him to see if he can pull any strings."

We both got up and marched down to the Skipper's office. When we arrived at his office, we presented our case to the Skipper as if we were famous lawyers pleading a lawsuit in court.

The Skipper thought for a while, stood up, and offered. "I think I have the perfect solution. I have a big box at home. Why don't I put you two in it, tie a ribbon around it and mail you to Florida?"

"That's not fair, Skipper. Maybe you could just lend us a couple of planes to use. I am sure we can find someone coming back this way to return them."

"OK, there is a shuttle service here, I'll see if I can get you two on it. In fact, Admiral Dean is here from the East coast. I was his aide at one time; I think he would let you ride along if I asked him to. I will try to contact him. Check with me before you go home this afternoon."

We both thanked the Skipper and told him we would see him later before we went home.

When we went back to see the Skipper, he told us that the Admiral had his headquarters in Jacksonville and would be happy to have you ride along with him. I'll give you his number so you can get with his aide and set things up.

We thanked the Skipper and headed to the Officer's Club for a couple of drinks before dinner. I remarked to Stan that everything was falling into place. We were off to a good start with our new jobs.

CHAPTER II

The time remaining at our old squadron seemed to evaporate into the air. We had been given a grand going-away party by our old squadron mates that were to stay with the old group. It was a sad and happy parting. We had been through a lot together and knew we had a lot ahead of us that could part us forever, but no one wanted to talk about that. It would find a dark corner in our mind and remain there, only to creep out in the loneliness of the night. Manifesting itself in haunting dreams that would relentlessly pursue you for the rest of your life.

The next morning, Stan and I were at the Admiral's plane early with our bags ready to throw on the airplane. When the Admiral arrived, he offered us a handshake and a pleasant good morning. After entering the plane, the Admiral's aide showed us to our seats. The Admiral would be seated ahead of us with a small desk to work at. When the Admiral boarded the plane, he motioned Stan and me to come forward and sit with him.

An enjoyable conversation followed with The Admiral asking our opinion on many issues. He was impressed with our combat records and showed a very eager interest in my time as a German prisoner. Both Stan and I were very impressed with the Admiral and thanked him profusely for allowing us to hitch a ride with him.

The flight to Jacksonville appeared to be rather short with the conversation we were engrossed in. When we landed, the Admiral asked us if we would care to attend a dinner that evening, where a number of the squadron commanders and executive officers would attend. Both the air group commander and the base commander would be there. It was to be informal with an effort on the Admirals' part to get input on their opinions and observations of the current situation. It was merely an informative meeting. We, of course, graciously accepted, although we would prefer not to attend. We just couldn't say no to an invitation from an Admiral.

Stan and I checked in with the base duty officer and continued to our new quarters. We hurriedly dug out our dress blue uniforms and took them over to be cleaned and pressed. After doing this, we found our way to the VF-21 squadron headquarters. We stopped in the ready room and met some of the pilots we would be flying with. After this, we went down to the Skipper's office to report in.

After knocking at the door, we were told to come in. The Skipper was seated at his desk. We marched up to his desk, came to attention, and one at a time stated our rank and name along with that we were reporting for duty. The Skipper stood up, walked around his desk, and welcomed us to VF-21 with a handshake. What followed was a pleasant and casual conversation. Our new Skipper was Commander Waltz. He was a very impressive man with a lot of combat behind him. He seemed to be impressed with our flying experience and told us it would be beneficial for all the new pilots we have in the squadron.

We thought, since he would be there, we better tell him that the Admiral had invited us to the dinner this evening. At first, he was a little surprised, so we told him how it came about. He said he would look forward to seeing us there and that he would try to arrange it so we could be seated together. Unless, of course, the Admiral had made other arrangements. We again shook hands and left his office.

That evening, the dinner went well. The Admiral, however, had Stan and me sit with him at the head table. I think we were both a little nervous, but the Admiral was very pleasant to us and even introduced us to the rest of the guests.

After dinner, several officers gave a presentation. We were asked to contribute our experiences and answered questions about what we thought of the view from someone who is on the front line.

The next morning, after we ventured down to where VF-21 had its headquarters, all the pilots had meetings with the Skipper to determine what their collateral duty would be. I ended up with being head of the maintenance department and Stan head of squadron safety.

Now we would start our indoctrination to the F8. After that, flight leaders would be chosen. They, in turn, would establish who would be in their flights. For a short time, we would rotate flying with different pilots to determine who worked best with whom. We would then start a concentrated effort to prefect our flying within our group.

The F8 was a magnificent airplane to fly. Small. Fast. And it could climb like a homesick angel. It was designed to combat the Japanese Kamikaze and could climb to 10,000 feet in less than two minutes. I am not sure there was another airplane in the world that could perform as it did. It would be a tremendous advantage for us.

After landing our flight one afternoon, we had noticed for all pilots to report to the ready room at 0400 hours. At 0400, every pilot in the squadron was at his seat in the ready room, wondering what was going on.

As the Skipper strolled into the ready room, all pilots came to attention. "At ease gentlemen, we received word an hour ago that the United States has dropped an atomic bomb on Japan. This bomb is something new and secret that, until now, most of us could not even comprehend its deadliness. They do not know the results, but it is thought it will have killed thousands and completely obliterated the Japanese city of Hiroshima. We will get a further report when more is known. We have issued a message to the Japanese leaders calling for unconditional surrender. I will let you know when I know more."

After the Skipper left, all the pilots just sat motionless for a long time. Finally, someone broke the silence, "What is an atomic bomb."

Someone offered, "I think I heard a little something about it. Something to do with splitting the atom."

Someone offered, "What kind of bomb could kill thousands?"

"I'm not sure, but it must have been a dandy."

We heard a lot of news about it in the next few days. Then three days later, we learned another had been dropped on Nagasaki with the same results.

We continued our training for the next several days. Then a Dispatch came in saying the Japanese had surrendered, followed in several more days by an order for us to suspend training until further notice. It did permit us to do some flying to get our necessary flight time in so we could draw our flight pay.

No one was sure of what would take place now that the Japanese had surrendered. We knew that the Navy would make drastic cuts in its manpower if the war were over. They certainly would not require all the pilots they had. We all were speculating on what would take place.

We lived in limbo for the next two months as we watch the Navy slim down to a shadow of what it had been. A lot of the pilots in VF-21 were given a chance to leave the Navy without any further obligation for service not served. Many accepted this out so they could return to civilian life and pursue what they had been trained in school for. A lawyer, teacher, accountant, or anything of a hundred or more careers. Stan had a degree in forestry, but he preferred to stay in the Navy. I had not finished college, so I wanted to do what I loved. That was flying.

Stan was allowed to stay in the Navy since he had a degree which the Navy felt would make him a better officer. I was told that since I did not possess a degree and had been injured, I would not be offered a career opportunity.

I was bitter. I didn't have a degree, but I knew I was a good pilot. They did offer me a reduction in rank, and I would be allowed to serve in the training command training new pilots. They would not need a lot of new pilots, but some had to be trained for future openings as the current pilots grew older.

Stan was my best friend. I could see in his eyes, his willingness to do what he could to help me. He said to me. "Bob, if you don't stay in, I won't either."

"Stan, if you do that, I will never speak to you again. You have the opportunity to shape a new Navy. You can and will make a difference. Just let me be your friend. If you do that, I will still be part of the Navy. Just be my friend, and I will be the luckiest man in the world. Who knows, someone may start another war, and they will need me again. We will always stay close."

"Why don't you and I go to the club tonight and celebrate the opportunities before us?"

"Bob, I will do that if you let me buy the first drink."

"Stan, you drive a hard bargain, but I will take you up on that if I can buy the last drink, and I decide when it is the last drink."

"You're on; let's go."

The night proved to be rather exciting and dangerous. I am not sure how we got home. I think someone took pity on us and drove us home. I know I didn't have to get dressed in the morning since I still had my uniform on. I think I was minus my hat and tie, but I wasn't like Stan, who lost both his shoes and both socks. The morning was a rather gloomy morning with the rain coming down in buckets. That just happened to be lucky for us. We called the squadron and was told all flying had been canceled, and we would not need to report in. I think the Skipper had gotten wind of our adventures the night before and was just being kind to us. I think he knew how I felt and turned his head the other way.

I had a lot of time throughout the day to think about what I would do. I knew I couldn't accept a reduction in rank and shoved to the back of the line, which was the training command. It wouldn't be so bad if I had held my rank and would be in the training command for just a short time, I could accept that, but not this. I was very bitter. I had given the Navy a large part of my life and almost my life. Now I was being thrown away like a dirty shirt.

All day long, it kept eating at me. If I were to leave the Navy, it would be with a proper goodbye. One that I would choose.

I arose early the next morning and watched the sun come up and hover on the horizon. The first rays appeared to be like arrows from under the earth, shooting through the sky, aiming at an elusive nonexistent enemy. It was like my enemy. I wasn't sure who or what it was, but I was angry and needed to vent my anger at someone or something. I need revenge, a revenge to satisfy my anger, a revenge to punish someone for what the Navy had done to me. First, I must choose my weapon, a weapon I knew how to use. It did not take me long to decide that the only weapon I knew how to use was an airplane.

I put my flight suit on and started to go out the door of our quarters. Stan heard me and asked what I was doing. "Stan, I am just going out for a breath of fresh air."

"Bob, it's not even 0600, why don't you wait a while and I will go with you."

"Try to get some more sleep, Stan. I don't think I can."

"Is something wrong, Bob."

"What could be wrong on such a beautiful day?"

"Bob, you're acting strangely. Are you all right?"

"I just need to get out and think about what I am going to do if I leave the Navy."

"Just don't do anything foolish, Bob."

"I'll see you later, Stan. Go back to sleep."

I walked outside and started for the airfield. The Sun was now above the horizon; its rays had all but disappeared, leaving a faint glow around it. I continued to the hanger area, which held some of our planes while some stood silently on the ramp bathed in the glow of the Sun.

When I reached the hanger, I saw our line chief, who was instructing his men in their duties. I walked over to him. "Chief, do you have a plane ready to fly?"

"Yes, sir, number two-zero-two, is ready."

"Get someone out there with an extinguisher to help me get started. Have him bring a Mae West when he comes out. Is there a chute in the plane?"

"Yes, sir, I will have someone right out."

I approached the plane and marveled at its beauty. What a beautiful beast. I pre-flighted the plane and took the Mae West the lineman handed me. I stepped up on the wing and climbed into the cockpit. The lineman helped me strap my chute on and took his position by the nose of the plane with his fire extinguisher. He gave me a thumbs up, telling me he was ready for me to start the engine.

The engine groaned as I hit the starter. The big four-bladed prop started a lazy movement and jumped into life, with smoke and fire belching from the cowling. It was like a dragon roaring to announce his power and authority. When it was running smoothly, I signaled the lineman to pull the chocks that held the wheels captive.

As I taxied out of the parking area, I could see someone walking toward me, stop, and turn around. I think it may have been Stan, but I didn't want to talk to him right now.

I called the tower and received the duty runway and further taxi instructions. When I reached the duty runway, I stopped long enough to see that the engine was running correctly. I had 2,000 horsepower under that cowling, and I wanted to be sure it was running correctly, and all the gauges were in the right place. I checked the controls for free movement, and the magnetos to be sure all spark plugs were doing their job. Lastly, I checked the engine RPM to make sure I could control the propeller. I gave the tower a call and announced that I was ready for takeoff. I was cleared onto the duty runway and cleared for takeoff. I taxied onto the runway, stopped for a moment, advanced the throttle to full throttle, and started my takeoff run. The engine roared as it went to full power and was in the air in a short distance. I pointed the nose up as I retracted the gear and headed toward the heavens. I soon was passing 5,000 feet and going over 200 knots. I had a feeling I was going home. I realized my home was in the sky, and I would find a way to make that a reality. I leveled off at 8,000 feet and let the speed build to 300 knots. I couldn't help but do two slow rolls in succession. That was followed by every maneuver I knew how to do.

There was no doubt now; I was home. I was like a carefree leaf floating around in a private world. A world I currently owned and would never relinquish. I could see the Sun in the east displaying all its glory. The arrows of sunlight had been replaced with a flood of light that chased the darkness into hiding and bid it not return till its allocated time. That time would be ruled by the Emperor, who was the Sun. He alone had that power given to him by God when he created the universe. Only God could change that. Until that time, his Majesty, the Sun, would rule our heavens.

I relapsed further into thought. I wondered why I had been allowed to live when so many had not. I had been in accidents that could easily have resulted in my death. I thought about the times Fred, my German guard, had pulled me out of a group of war prisoners that were going to be shot. Now Fred was dead. After all, he did for me; I could not help him when he needed me most. Now I was also denied staying in the Navy and flying. I wanted that so badly, and yet it was taken from me. Maybe I am destined to do something else. I wish I knew. I have lost control, and I'm in freefall. I don't have any idea where that freefall will land me. I vowed to put myself in God's hands and ask him to let me make a difference. I want mostly to help people, those that are suppressed and victimized by someone or something. I want to make a difference.

I came back to reality and decided I better go back to the base. As I was letting down, I had the thought that I should do something to commemorate my last flight in a Navy airplane. I called the tower. "Jacksonville tower, this is F8 two-zero-two, requesting landing instructions and clearance for a low high-speed pass."

"Two-zero-two, the duty runway is three-six, negative on the high-speed pass."

"Tower, this is two-zero-two, this is probably my last flight in the Navy. I again request a high-speed pass."

"Two-zero-two, it's not in the regulations, I am not allowed to do that."

"Tower, this is two-zero-two, I think I am having a problem with my landing gear. Request a flyby so you can check my gear for down and locked."

"Two-zero-two, we can do that, you are cleared for a flyby to check your gear."

"Roger, Tower, I will do a flyby from South to North."

"Roger, two-zero-two."

I couldn't help thinking, I know I shouldn't do this, but the most they can do is kick me out of the Navy. I think they are doing that already, so I don't have a lot to lose. I was at 4,000 feet, so I dropped down to 1,500 feet and flew south until I was about ten miles from the field. I cleaned the airplane up by closing the cowl flaps and started my letdown. At five miles out, I was approaching over 300 knots with the throttle not quite fully forward. I was down to 800 feet. I open the throttle to the full position and started down. As I approach the field, I planned to be over the runway at about ten feet high. As I approached the runway, I was going well over 300 knots.

I was going so fast the tower was almost a blur, and I was some twenty or thirty feet below its top.

As I pulled up, I called the tower. "Tower, did you get a good look at my landing gear?"

"Two-zero-two, all we saw was a blur going by, you need to slow down a bit, so we have time to look at them."

"Roger, Tower. I must have been below you so you couldn't see them. I will make another pass and roll inverted so you can get a good look."

Two-zero-two, I can't clear that. You are on your own."

"Roger, Tower, I understand that."

The next pass, I came in just as fast and did two slow rolls as I was going down the runway.

"Two-zero-two, I can tell you that your landing gear is not down."

"Roger, Tower. I will try to correct that."

"Two-zero-two, if you will check it out, I think you have dignitaries among a large number of spectators. I believe one is the Captain of the base. I am sure he may want to congratulate you on your stunning performance. I think he wants to talk to you. He is on the radio now."

"Roger, Tower, thank you for that bit of information."

"Lieutenant Baker, this is Captain Roberts, I am ordering you to land that plane immediately."

"Aye Aye, Sir, will do."

I was sure I was in a heap of trouble. Somehow I didn't care what the higher-ups did, they had already taken away what I wanted most, so I can't think of anything they can do to punish me anymore.

I landed and taxied up to our hanger and parked my airplane. Stan was there with some Shore Patrol officers. Stan spoke first. "Bob, what in the world got into you? You know they will probably take your wings for this."

"Stan, they already have. I don't think they can hurt me anymore than they have already."

"Bob, I don't want to see you go out this way."

"Doesn't make any difference, Stan. I'll be on the outside looking in no matter what happens. I hope you can accept what I did and remain my friend."

"There is no question about that, Bob. I don't know of anything that could change that. I'm with you no matter what happens. I may leave the Navy also after what they did to you."

"Don't do that. One fool is enough to handle right now. I don't care what they do to me, as long as they don't throw me in the brig."

We walked up to the hanger, escorted by the Shore Patrol. The Skipper was standing there to meet us. I just said, "Sorry, Skipper."

The Skipper just looked at me and shook his head. "Bob, what in the world got into you?"

"The Navy has decided to get rid of me or make me quit. I just wanted to sing my swan song."

"I am sure you did a good job of that, Bob, I'll be in your corner no matter what happens. Believe that you can count on me for my full support."

"Thank you, Skipper, but I don't want to drag you down. One of us is enough."

I looked at the Shore Patrol and then the Skipper. "Are these guys going to throw me in the brig?"

"I won't let that happen, Bob. You didn't break any laws; you just went off the deep end for a short time. By the way, which was some show you put on. I was impressed. I hope someone filmed that; I would like to see it again."

"If you loan me an airplane, I would be happy to do it again."

"I think once is enough, Bob. Why don't you go home and relax for now? You're free to do what you want, no confinement to quarters. You and I will get together tomorrow morning. I want to speak to the base commander. He needs to know the full story."

"Don't stick your neck out too far, Skipper."

"Stan, stick with this guy. Don't let him out of your sight. I'll see you in the morning, Bob."

CHAPTER III

The next morning found Stan and me in the Officer's Mess having breakfast. Some of the other pilots from VF-21 were there also. All were friendly, but no one mentioned what happened yesterday. Most of the conversation was about the weather or other menial things. Some wished me good luck in whatever I chose to do after I left the Navy. Some asked me what I planned to do when I got back home. Most wished me well.

I knew I had to face the Skipper this morning, which was not a pleasant thought.

After breakfast, Stan asked if I wanted him to go with me. I told him it was my fight, and I did not want him to get involved. I told him nothing good could come of it, so it was best he stayed away. He just told me he would do whatever I wanted him to do. I thanked him and told him again. I appreciated his offer, but it would be best for him to stay out of it.

After we arrived at the squadron, Stan went to the ready room, and I headed for the Skipper's office. I knocked on the door and was told to come in. I didn't say anything as I walked into the room. The Skipper just told me to come in and have a seat.

"Bob, I talked to Admiral Dean yesterday. He wants you to come over to his office. I told him I would send you over as soon as you came in. I don't know what he wants. He just said to send you over."

"I guess the Navy may be coming down harder on me than I thought they would. I better go face the music."

"I will help in any way I can, Bob. I don't think I can override an Admiral, though. Let me know if you think I can help in any way."

I will Skipper, thanks for the offer."

With that, I left the room and started for the Admiral's office.

I was more than a little nervous as I started over to Admiral Dean's office. I was wondering why I did that fool trick yesterday. I should have just left quietly and let it go at that.

I approached the Admiral's aide and told him I was there to see the Admiral. He asked if I had an appointment. "No, I was just told the Admiral wanted to see me."

"Wait here, and I will see if the Admiral will see you."

After the Aide spoke to the Admiral, I was told to go in, the Admiral would see me. I nervously got up and walked in. I stood in front of his desk at attention and told him I was reporting as ordered.

"Have a seat, Lieutenant." I was taken aback. I could not understand why the Admiral had me sit down if I was going to get reprimanded.

"I know you must think that you are here because of what happened yesterday. In a way, you are, but there is more to it than that. This is top secret, so if you do or don't accept my offer, it can only be discussed with me or someone I designate. Can you accept those terms?"

"Yes, sir, I can and do."

"There is an organization in South America made up of German Nazis who we think may have escaped with some of Hitler's top-secret experiments, as well as a fortune in gold, jewels, and artwork. We think some of these experiments are capable of mass destruction in material or lives. They have several pilots and planes as well as ground weapons. They are protected by the government of the country they are in, so we cannot just go in and take them with force. We are sure they plan to retaliate with these weapons at some point. Here is where you come in. We have a small friendly island country that will allow us to use their country to capture or destroy the before mentioned weapons before they can use them against us. The Nazis want this island to work from with more privacy. It will be necessary for us to appear to be working with that country with supplies to protect them. We have given them ten P-51 Mustang fighters to use for their protection. Their pilots will be volunteer pilots from different countries, and they know nothing about our true intervention. If you accept, you will be in charge of the pilots and aircraft. You will be discharged from the Navy with an honorable discharge to avoid any connection with our military. You will be paid $10,000 a month by the people you are working for, and also, you will receive a like amount from us to be paid at a later date. This, I assure you, will happen. They may strike a deal with you for a lesser amount, but the figure I gave you will be the one you will receive."

"Bob, there is a lot of risk in this for you. It is quite certain that you could be in combat situations. I think you know what I am saying. Think about it, and let me know what you decide."

"I don't need to think about it. I will welcome my chance to serve my country."

"I was sure you would say that. You're that kind of man. You can still back out before we get started if you wish."

"I won't back out, Sir. I do have one question, or maybe it is a request."

"Go ahead."

"If I survive, will I be allowed to go back into the Navy with my same rank after this is completed?"

"Bob, I think I can make that happen. No! I know I can make that happen."

"Thank you, sir."

"We will avoid contact with each other. I will contact you in different ways to avoid any suspicion. Good luck, and may God be with you."

I left the Admiral's office with my head spinning. I wondered what I had gotten myself into.

When I arrived back at our squadron, I was greeted by Stan and was asked how it went.

"Stan, you won't believe it. I pictured myself going before a firing squad. The Admiral was nice to me. I think he understood how I felt. I will be allowed to leave the Navy with an honorable discharge. A comment on what I did will be entered into my record without a reprimand. I think I got lucky."

"I think you got double lucky. You must have done something right."

"I don't think our meeting him before hurt me. He must have considered my record and gave me a break."

I thought I had said enough, and better just leave it there.

I put in a request for my release from active duty and discharge from the Navy. I was told it would take a few weeks, so all I could do was wait. I wanted to get a handbook on the P-51; however, I thought that was not the smartest thing to do.

I did get a message from someone that I would be contacted by a representative from the country in South America I was to help. Stan and I were at a little bar in town one evening when a stranger came in and started to talk to us. He asked if he could join us, so we told him to have a seat.

The conversation started this way. "You boys look like pilots, is that right?"

Stan answered. "We are, we are Navy pilots. Why do you ask?"

"Just curious. Actually, I am from South America. My country needs experienced pilots to help train our small air force. Do you know anyone that may be interested, the pay is pretty good?"

"How good?" I asked.

"Depends on your experience. It starts at $1,000 a month, and if you have a lot of experience, it could go as high as $1,500 a month."

I answered. "You have my attention. Go on."

The stranger smiled. "Tell me what your experience is, and I can give you a figure and more information.

I smiled right back. "I have about five years in the Navy, seven planes shot down, and seven months in a German prison camp."

"Wow, do you have any leadership experience?"

"I was in charge of squadron operations at one time. I thought I was being groomed for command. The answer is, yes, I have leadership experience and can handle it."

"What is your rank?"

"I am a senior Lieutenant. I assume, because of the war, I would be up soon for Lieutenant Commander."

"Lieutenant, I will give you a phone number to call. They will be able to answer all your questions." I will talk to them first, so they will know I have spoken to you and recommend you. You can give them my code name, which is "Fred." That way, they will know who you are."

When he said Fred, I almost knocked my drink over. I was stunned for a short time, then I asked. "How did you get the name, Fred?"

"It's a long story. Fred was a very close friend of mine who is no longer with us. He was special to me. He saved my life in a boating accident."

For a few moments, I was stunned and couldn't speak. Finally, I offered, "I had a very close friend by the name of Fred. He saved my life while I was a German prisoner. He died in my arms."

"Lieutenant, maybe that is an omen. I would like to think it is."

"Maybe so."

"I would like to tell you more about our people, Lieutenant. We inhabit an island about a hundred miles from the mainland and number about 100,000. We are all God-fearing people who prefer to live our life the way we choose. There are German survivors on the mainland that want to take over our country. I know they are evil people and would savage our land and our people. In short, they would destroy our way of life and more or less make our people subject to them. We have a small army, but very little resources to protect ourselves from them, but we will try."

He hesitated for a minute or so and continued. Your government has given us guns for our protection and also ten Mustang fighters. We have hired six pilots from various countries to fly them and some specialists to maintain them. We do still need someone to lead them. We want someone who understands our cause and will help us."

He hesitated again. We have a strong President to guide us, but his strength and our willingness are not enough. We need someone who understands how to operate militarily. I am hoping it will be you. We have a strong leader. Now we need a strong man to show us how to survive."

He hesitated a third time. "It won't be easy, and we know that people may die. I don't think I need to tell you that after hearing what you have already been through. Our enemy has already tried to kill our President, and I know they will try again. They are very evil people that escaped from Germany and taken refuge in a neighboring country that we are not friendly with. With God's help, we will survive, but we need help. We are asking you to be that help."

"I am overwhelmed, may I call you Fred?"

"Please do. Do you have a name?"

"Yes, it is Bob."

"Bob, the phone number I gave you is to a member of our government. He can and will answer all your questions. I will tell him and our president about you. I know they will both welcome you to our country."

"Fred, I will give it a lot of serious thought. For once in my life, I can't come up with an answer right now.

"Take your time, Bob, this is not an easy decision."

Fred stood up, shook hands with both of us, and departed.

Stan looked at me with a curious look."

"Are you seriously considering flying for that country?"

"I am, Stan. I would really like to fly the P-51."

"Are you out of your mind, Bob? People get killed doing things like that."

"People get killed doing what you will also be doing."

It wasn't a tough decision to make since I had already committed to it with Admiral Dean. I did have to make it look like I was interested before a commitment to the country was created.

I waited two days to make it look good before I called the number Fred had given me. A woman's voice in Spanish greeted me on the other end. "This is Lieutenant Baker, do you speak English?"

"I do, Lieutenant, how may I direct your call?"

"A gentleman by the name of Fred gave me this phone number and told to call it."

"Please hold on, Lieutenant, I will connect you to someone who can help you."

"Thank you."

After a short pause, I heard. "What can I do for you, Lieutenant?"

"I was given this phone number by a gentleman by the name of Fred and told to call it."

"Thank you for calling, Lieutenant, I am Marcos, and do assist President Villa. I assume you are calling about a flying position."

"I am, Marcos."

"I am certain Fred told you about our program here in Rutland."

"He briefly explained it to me."

"How much did he tell you, Lieutenant?"

"Fred told me you were having a problem with some people who would like to take over your country, and they were a threat to you. He also filled me in what you had for airplanes, and what you have acquired so far. He also told me you needed help in putting this program together and training the pilots."

"That is completely correct, Lieutenant. Fred told us a lot about you and your experiences. He said you were a Navy pilot with a lot of enemy planes shot down, and that you had been a German prisoner in France."

"I think that covers it pretty much, Marcos."

"What would you like to know, Lieutenant?"

"I would like to know what the opposition is flying, how many planes they have, and how many pilots."

"That's a fair question. They are flying the ME-109, have approximately fifteen planes and, we think, between twelve and fifteen pilots."

"Do you know how experienced the pilots are, Marcos?"

"Not for sure. We think probably about half are fairly well experienced, and the rest in various degrees of experience. We know that some of the experienced have a lot of combat experience, and there are some aces among them. If I understand what an ace is."

"An ace has five or more aerial victories. Victories are planes shot down."

"That is what I was told, Lieutenant."

"I have been up against the ME-109 many times. I have two to my credit."

"That is what Fred had told us, along with five Japanese Zeros."

"Correct, I think the German pilots were better pilots because Japan lost a lot of their best pilots using them for Kamikaze attacks."

"Bob, you will command a high salary. That I can guarantee you. Our president would like very much to meet and talk with you."

"As you know, Marcos, travel is not very easy right now, especially foreign travel."

"Bob, we do not have the other pilots here yet. They are waiting for us to act first. We do have some of the planes here. The rest are still in Florida at an Air Force base. Can you go there and fly one down? You can fly it back when you leave."

"I think I can do that if I can get some time off here. I haven't been discharged yet, so I will have to come back. I haven't flown the P-51 yet, so I may see if I can get a couple of hops in before I leave. If the Air Force is Eglin, I am close. I think the Skipper will let me borrow an F8 to go there."

"I will make the arrangements, Bob. I will have someone contact you tomorrow and give you the go-ahead. If you can work it out with your Skipper, let our contact know. When you do feel comfortable with the P-51, tell the contact, and we will set it up for you to fly down."

"Thanks, Marcos, I will get things going here and wait for your contact to talk to me."

"I look forward to seeing you, Lieutenant. I am very excited about it."

"I must admit I am too; I will see you soon." I hung the phone up and sat bewildered with my head spinning.

I talked to the skipper later that day and asked if I could use a plane to fly to Eglin Air Force base. I did give him a briefing on what was going down. "I may have to get some clearance from higher up to make that available to you, Bob."

"Skipper, I would like this to be low key. I will need to borrow a plane again to fly a P-51 down there for a couple of days."

"I guess I can stick my neck out for you, Bob. I can have you pick something up both times. I just need to figure out what it will be. I will think of something. Just don't tell anyone what is truly going on, will you?"

"I can do that, Skipper. Stan does know what I am doing; it might be best to tell him, so he doesn't say anything."

"Probably a good idea. Let me know when you will be going, and I will arrange things here."

"Thanks, Skipper." I left the Skipper's office and started my journey into the unknown.

CHAPTER IV

Stan and I were sitting in our quarters, having a beer when the phone rang. I picked it up and greeted the caller with a hello.

"Is this Bob?" I recognized the voice as that of Fred. "It is, is this Fred?"

"It is, Bob. I have everything all set for you to go to Eglin Air Force base and fly one of our P–51 Mustangs."

"Thanks, Fred, I should be able to go over there tomorrow. Do I need to let them know I am coming?"

"They said for you to come over anytime, and they would get you checked out."

"Sounds good, Fred, I will let you know how things are going and when I will be going to see your President."

"Do that. Good luck." And Fred hung up.

The next morning, I stepped into the Skipper's office to tell him I was cleared to go to Eglin and asked if it would be all right if I went today.

"That should be fine. Let me know when you get back."

"I will do that, Sir."

I Stopped long enough to file a flight plan and started for the F8 I had told them to get ready for me. It took me only a short time to preflight my plane. After the preflight was complete, I climbed into the F8, started it, got my taxi instructions, and continued on my way.

After I was in the air, I continued West until I saw the Gulf of Mexico. I then called Eglin tower." Eglin Tower, this is Navy two-zero-six, over."

"Roger, two-zero-six, this is Eglin Tower."

"Roger, Tower, I will be over Eglin in about fifteen minutes, request landing instructions."

"Roger, two-zero-six. The duty runway is three, two. Contact us before you enter the break for landing."

"Roger, Tower, will do. Will you notify the duty officer that Lieutenant Baker is arriving for indoctrination in the P-51 and ask them to notify the proper people?"

"Roger, two-zero-six, we can do that."

It wasn't long before I saw the airfield. "Eglin Tower, this is Navy two-zero-six; I will be in the break in three minutes."

"Roger, two-zero-six, you are cleared into the break, and cleared for landing."

"Roger, Tower."

About halfway down the runway at 500 feet, I made a sharp turn to the left and closed my throttle. I allowed my plane to decelerate until I reached the speed at which I could lower my landing gear. By this time, I had turned 180 degrees onto my downwind leg, which was parallel to the runway, and opposite the direction of landing. As the gear came down and locked, I descended to 300 feet and added power to maintain my altitude. I then dropped my flaps to slow me down further. I kept a wingtip distance to the runway until I reached the end of the runway. I started a slow descending turn to the left, allowing my speed to drop to 85 knots. As I came over the end of the runway, I closed the throttle and started to flair for a smooth touch down.

As the plane continued to roll out and lose speed, the tower called telling me which taxiway to use and directed me to where I would park.

It was then that I saw a large number of people watching me. It occurred to me that they had never seen an F8 before and were very curious. I was guided into my parking spot and shut my plane down.

An Air Force Captain met me with a handshake and a welcome to Eglin Air Force base.

"Good morning, Lieutenant. Welcome to Eglin. I will be the one to work with you."

"Thanks, Captain, I am anxious to fly the P-51."

"We can arrange that. Is this the Navy's new F8F, Lieutenant?"

"It is,"

"Looks like a mean machine to me."

"It is an awesome animal. On the same level as your P-51."

"I wish I could fly it."

"I wish I could let you, but I think you know the rest of the story."

"I'm afraid I do, Lieutenant. I understand you only have a couple of days, so we will get right to it. First, I want to go over all the mechanics and characteristics." We started for a hanger and selected a room he had prepared for us.

We spent about two hours going over everything he could think of about the P-51. He had a P-51 in the hanger that we used for the hands-on part.

In questioning him, I found out he had flown the P-51 in combat and shot down three German planes. I was very impressed with him and the way he conducted himself. I had no doubt he was an awesome fighter pilot.

The time came for me to fly it. Two P-51s sat in the parking area, one with U.S. markings, the other with none. It was obvious which one I would fly.

The Captain helped me start the engine and offered a few more suggestions. He stepped off the wing of my plane and walked over to the other P-51. After he had it started, he called me asking me if I was ready.

"Lieutenant, follow me out to the duty runway. After we do our runup to check the engine, I will have you take the runway. I will follow you and get into a formation takeoff position. I will stay with you in a loose position to give you a little breathing room. I will move in a little closer after we are in the air. Let me know if you are not comfortable with that."

"Roger, I never asked you your name. I hate to keep saying, Captain. My name is Bob."

"Bob, my name is Roger, but I go by Al, which is my middle name."

"OK, Al, you don't have to explain that one to me. I'm ready when you are."

Al called the tower and received clearance for takeoff. I taxied onto the duty runway and stopped with Al staying a short distance back and to my right.

"You all set, Al?"

All I heard was, "All set."

I advanced my throttle to the fully open position and pulled it back slightly so Al could stay with me. I raised my right hand and held it there. I received a thumbs up from Al, so I dropped my hand and released my brakes at the same time. That was the signal for Al to release his brakes. We rolled down the runway together. As I lifted off the runway, I saw Al do the same. I raised my landing gear and watched as Al did likewise.

"Bob, that was a nice takeoff. Have you flown the P-51 before?"

"Al, compliments will get you nowhere, I will buy you a drink at the club anyway."

"You mean I don't have to be nice to you?"

"I didn't say that, Al."

"OK, Bob, I will break off from you so you can get the feel of the beast."

"Good, I will let you know when I am ready to go back."

"Bob, switch to channel 12 so we can get off the tower frequency."

I just came back with a "Roger."

For the next thirty minutes, I ran the P-51 through its paces to get the feel of it. It performed beautifully. I could see why it achieved the fame it had in combat. I continued getting the feel of the P-51 for another forty-five minutes. I then decided to shoot a few touch-and-go landings. I contacted Al and told him I was ready to go back to the base. Al acknowledged that he was ready anytime I was ready.

"I will join up on you so we can go in together."

"Roger, Bob. I'll go into a slow left turn so you can join on me. What did you think of it, Bob?"

"Al, this airplane is great. I wish I could let you fly the F8."

"I wish I could too, Bob. Maybe another time."

"Let's head over to the club, Al. I will buy you a drink. I want more input on this beautiful bird too."

"Sounds like a deal, Bob."

The rest of the flight was uneventful. We landed and strolled over to the Officer's club for refreshments.

We arrived at the club a little early, so we had the place pretty much to ourselves. We had a good conversation telling each other about our experiences and our families. The Martinis were going down much too easy. At one point, I stopped and just looked at Al. I knew I was going to regret what I was about to say.

"Al, would you really like to fly the F8?"

"Bob, don't tease me, please."

"I'm not. You are one heck of a good pilot; you just got mixed up and went into the wrong service. I need to make you an honorary Navy pilot. I don't know how you can be an honorary Navy pilot if you never flew a Navy airplane. We need to correct the mistakes of the past. Tomorrow morning, we will make that correction and let you feel what a real Navy pilot feels like."

"I don't have to land on an aircraft carrier, do I, Bob? If I do, I will need to get a few more drinks in me."

"I can tell you never landed on a carrier and don't know the secret of how to do that."

"I'm all ears."

"Don't tell any navy pilot I told you this. It is the secret known only among Navy pilots."

"I'm still listening."

I leaned over as if to whisper in Al's ear. When you see the signal officer give you the cut, that is the signal to shut your eyes."

"Wow! I didn't know that. Tell me what that does for you."

"It prevents you from seeing the accident."

We eventually wrapped up the meeting with a promise to meet for breakfast at 0700.

The next morning found Al waiting for me at the Officer's Mess hall.

"Bob, the first thing I want to say is that I will not hold you to your promise last night. It was obtained in a very devious way,"

"Al, I am a man of my word. What I promised will happen. After breakfast, we will go down to the hanger and make you a Navy pilot."

We did do just that. I was biting my nails a little, but Al was a great pilot, and all went well. I did make him swear to secrecy after we landed. I, in turn, got more flight time in the P-51.

Just before I left, I approached Al. "I would like something from you if you will do it."

"What is that, Bob."

"I told you a little of what I would be doing in the future in South America."

"Yes, you did."

"When I come back and get a P-51 to fly to South America, I think there is a chance I will run into hostile planes. I don't want to do that with unloaded guns. I think you can guess the rest."

"That doesn't take much of a guess, Bob. How do you want the guns loaded?"

"Can you get me the standard load for aerial combat, like an armor-piercing, tracer, high explosive, and incendiary rounds?"

"I can do that, Bob. A good friend is in charge of our weapons. I don't think I will have any trouble. What will you be up against?"

"ME-109s."

"When you come back to go down to South America, let me know ahead of time. Try to get here so you can stay overnight. I want you to meet my wife. If you don't mind. Her sister is here. I would like you to meet her. It would be an honor for both of them."

"I would like to meet them. Just don't tell them too much about what I will be doing. It is really not for publication."

"I understand."

Al walked down to my plane with me. As I climbed in, he gave me a salute. I saluted him back.

The flight back to Jacksonville was uneventful. I tried to digest all that had taken place in the last few weeks. It all began to seem like a dream, a dream I had a hard time making become a reality. I just now started to wonder what I was getting myself in for. If I survive, it will undoubtedly be an experience beyond anything I could imagine. Suddenly, I began to wonder if I would survive whatever was in store for me. I sank deeper into my mystical world, telling myself that I should be pursuing a normal life. I should find some nice girl, get married and have a family. Instead, I was going from one life of jeopardy into another. I began to wonder if I was a little insane. If I enjoyed living on the edge.

I sat in a sort of daze for a long time. I wondered if I could blame my love of flying for the actions I was taking. Did the thrill of combat give me some sort of high? I vowed to look for a valid reason for me to do what I was doing. I promised myself that if I could not place a valid reason on it, I would hang it up and quit. Secretly, I was afraid I would concoct a reason and call that valid. I vowed to myself that I would not do that. It had to be valid enough for me to risk my life for.

Suddenly, I was jolted back to reality when another F8 slid into formation with me. The pilot just gave me a thumbs up and signaled me to switch my radio to channel nine. There was little doubt about who it was. I could not see his face because he had his oxygen mask on. I did, however, recognize him by his helmet. Stan had some unusual markings on it, which left little doubt about who it was. "Good afternoon, Stan, it was nice of you to escort me back to the base. How did you find me?"

"I saw the flight plan you had filed. I checked with Air Traffic Control to see where you were at. The rest was easy. What do you think of the P-51?"

"Stan, it is a great plane, on a level with the F8. I can see why it received the notoriety it did. The F8 can out climb it, but the P-51 handles beautifully. The range is unbelievable, and with a drop tank, it is even more unbelievable. I love it."

"Is it worth risking your life to fly?"

"Funny, you should ask. I was just pondering that question on my way back."

"Did you find an answer?"

"Not yet, but I need to."

"Bob, I can't imagine you will find one."

"I'm going to South America in a few days, I will let you know what, and if, I found a reason."

"Do I get to vote on it?"

"Stan, you know I value your opinion. It may be so good that you will want to join me. I see the field. I am switching to the Tower frequency for landing instructions."

I switched to the Tower frequency and called for landing instructions. Stan stayed on my wing as I came into the break and landed.

When we walked into the hanger, we talked about other things. I thought to myself about what a good friend Stan is. I will miss him a lot. We have been together for a long time. After our conversation in the air, I again vowed to find a valid reason to go to South America, or I would not go.

I went to the Skipper's office to let him know I was back. The Skipper was overflowing with questions, so I had to answer the same basic questions I had been asked by Stan. I also received the same question of whether it was worth risking my life for. I gave the skipper the same answer I had given Stan.

In the next few days, Stan and I spent a lot of time together. I know Stan was avoiding question me further on my motives for what I was doing. He was not alone; I was questioning them myself. I think this was like a thing called buyer's remorse. After you have purchased a large item, it is not uncommon to wonder if you did the right thing. This was no different. Only the stakes were much higher. I did vow to let Stan be my sounding board. When I decided, I would run it by him to get his thoughts and opinion.

I contacted Fred and told him I had been checked out in the P-51 and was ready to meet his President.

Fred seemed pleased and offered. "Bob, I will get in contact with President Villa and set up a time for you to go to my country and meet him. I know you will be very impressed when you do meet."

"I am looking forward to going. I need to have some lead time, so I can have my plane readied. Let me know a couple of days ahead if you can."

"I will do that, Bob.

The next couple of days seemed to drag by as I waited for an answer from Fred. All that time, I wondered what a valid reason would be for me to go through with this.

Fred's call finally came. "I have spoken to my people and found a date when he will be available. It will be next Monday if that will work for you?"

"I am sure it will, Fred. I will let you know if I need to change it."

I contacted Al at Eglin and ask if he would pass it on, and also reminded him to have the guns armed. He verified it and said he had already taken care of it. I also asked him if he could get a fuel drop tank for me. He said he could.

Everything was a go.

CHAPTER V

I decided to fly to Eglin a day early and spend some time with Al, his wife, and her sister. I thought it would be nice to spend a quiet evening and get an early start the next morning. I would fly to an island off the north coast of Venezuela. The distance was about 1,500 miles. I could fly this in five hours or less if I caught the right winds. With a drop tank, I should not have a problem flying that far. I think I could get my cruise speed up to over 300 miles per hour and stay in the air for over six hours. I may have to switch altitude to find the right tailwind, but I did not think that would be a problem. I would not take any extra clothes other than underclothing and socks. I don't think I would be there for more than a day or two. I would put in some snacks in case I got hungry.

One of my concerns was the weather. I didn't mind flying through it, but I did not know about their landing system. If they could get me to within a hundred feet of the ground, I can handle the rest. That was a chance I would have to take.

I called Al to tell him I would be there Saturday and fly out of Eglin very early Monday morning. I would take Sunday, after church, to get the plane ready, and leave early Monday. I would meet with the President on Monday afternoon. I asked Al if he thought he could put up with me for that long.

"That will not be a problem. You can stay longer if you prefer. You are more than welcome to stay over on your way back to Jacksonville."

"I don't think I have thought that far ahead at this point, Al. Maybe we can have a drink and dinner if I get back in time."

"I will plan on that, Bob. I will be very interested in what you have decided."

"I knew I would be flying over water much of the time I was in the air, so I wanted to be sure I had a good Mae West and a rubber boat in my chute. I knew they were in the parachute seat in my F8, so I would take that chute if it would fit into the P-51.

I don't know if I was excited to get on with the job or wondering if I did the wrong thing. At some point, I would know. That is if I was still alive.

I was getting nervous about this new adventure. I think I was starting to show it to Stan.

Stan did ask me if I thought I wanted to back out.

"No, Stan, I am not backing out. I committed, and I intend to see it through. I think anyone would be nervous about the prospects of a new job."

"Bob, it's not just a regular job. You can get killed with this job."

I just smiled at Stan and told him he was right. "Are you sure you don't want to go down with me, you might like it."

"I'll wait to see what you find out, but I am sure it will be a negative response."

The next few days passed rather slowly. I think I was starting to get a little nervous. Finally, Saturday did come. I gathered the few things I would take along and placed them in a small bag that I could put in the cockpit with me. I was up Saturday morning early. Not wanting to impose on Al, I took my time getting ready. About noon, I made my way to the squadron and asked if they had my plane ready. I received a positive response, so I leisurely checked my plane and prepared to go to Eglin.

By 0100, I was ready, so I decided to go. It would not take long to get to Eglin, so I was not in a hurry to call Al. I did call Al after I landed and asked if he would pick me up when he had time. "Bob, we have been waiting for you. I thought you would be here before now."

"I didn't want to impose on you, so I took my time. I still don't want to impose on you, so whenever you find the time, I will be at the base."

"I will be there in a few minutes, just hold tight."

"I don't think I will be going anywhere, so I will be here when you get here."

"Just stay put, I'll be there in fifteen minutes."

I didn't know Al, so I was not in too much of a hurry to impose on him. I was looking forward to seeing him again, but I didn't want to be overly forward.

Fifteen minutes went rather quickly. Al was there before I knew it. I saw him coming toward me as I stood in the hanger. When he approached, I heard a very welcome comment. "Bob, I have been looking forward to seeing you again. You better be prepared for two ladies that think you are some sort of conquering hero. I tried to play it down, but I was not too good at it. I think I have even convinced myself."

"Al, if I have to defend some sort of image you have portrayed, I think I better stay here."

"Bob, the image I have portrayed is that of a conquering hero. Someone who can walk on water."

"I'm not going, Al. I will sit out on the street curb, and you can bring me a ham and cheese sandwich."

"I am sorry to say that all your faithful subjects will follow me casting roses for you to walk on."

"I'm scared."

"I am afraid I didn't do that, Bob, but I do have two ladies that are looking forward to meeting you. I hope you won't disappoint them.

"I could never do that. I can honestly say I am looking forward to meeting both of them."

I enjoyed meeting Al's family. His wife, Sally, was a pretty, charming lady. Sally's sister, Pat, was just as charming and attractive as Sally. I was more than impressed with her. I instantly felt a warm feeling come over me as we shook hands. I couldn't help but say, "Pat, I'm afraid I am more of a hugger; do you mind?"

"Not at all, I'm afraid I am the same way." With that, I received a very warm and friendly hug.

I turned to Sally, "Sally, I am afraid I missed you." I, again, was the recipient of another warm and friendly hug from her.

The early afternoon was filled with a pleasant conversation, mostly about what I would be doing. Later, we decided to go to the Officer's Club for a drink and dinner. I did not bring a uniform, so Al loaned me something casual to wear.

After dinner, a small band showed up to provide some entertainment and dancing. Pat was an excellent dancer, so we did dance a lot. It was a great evening spent with some very charming people.

Al and Sally insisted that I stay overnight at their home and attend church with them in the morning. Which I graciously accepted.

The next morning, after church, we had breakfast at a cozy little restaurant near the base. After this, we adjourned to a patio at home to continue our conversation of the previous evening.

At about 1400 hours, I announced. "I think I better get my plane ready for tomorrow. I plan to get to bed early and get up about 0300, so I can take off by 0400 or 0430. I have a long way to go. I will be in the air for five hours or more. If I have favorable winds, I should not have to stop. If I do, I will try to get to a friendly country and refuel there. It could take another two or three hours if I had to. I want to be at my destination by mid-morning so that I can meet with the president in the early afternoon."

"If everything goes well, I will leave there early Tuesday and be back here around noon. I am due back in Jacksonville for Wednesday's work schedule. I am sure I won't be able to stay over on Tuesday. I may have time for coffee or lunch with you, Al. If the ladies are free, I would love to see them also. I will call the base on my way back and ask them to contact you with an estimated time of arrival."

"Bob, I will keep myself free Tuesday and look for your message. I want to know what went on and what you decided."

Pat entered the conversation. I would like to see you again, Bob, even if only for a short time. I wish you could stay longer."

"I do too, Pat. I know I can't on my way back, but maybe we can make it later. It all depends on what I decide to do."

"I hope you decide not to do that, it's far too dangerous, and I had hoped maybe we could get better acquainted."

"Pat, I will admit I have had some of the same thoughts."

"I don't think I will ever understand men and their silly way of trying to get killed. I don't want to get to like you so much right now. I didn't tell you, but I was engaged to a pilot friend of Al's, which did not end well. He lost his life over Germany."

"I am sorry to hear that, Pat."

"Just take care of yourself, Bob, and try not to get yourself killed."

"I will do that, Pat. Don't I at least get a hug goodbye?"

"If you think it will bring you back alive."

I stepped over to Pat and gave her not only a hug but also a very passionate kiss. "I think that might be even better."

Pat put her arms around me again and gave me an even more passionate kiss. "Two are better than one, Bob."

I said goodbye to Pat, hugged Sally, and walked out with Al.

At the base, we found my plane and checked it over. Everything was as it should be. It was now late in the afternoon, so I shook hands with Al while saying. "I will see you in two days. I can't thank you enough for your hospitality. I would like to see Pat again, but I think she is afraid of me and what could happen."

"You can't blame her, Bob, she had a bad experience before, and she doesn't want to repeat it."

I just told Al he was right and walked toward where I was to bunk for the night.

My alarm went off at 0300, which startled me. I got up, dressed in my flight suit, and started for the hanger my plane was in. I found the duty officer in his shack and asked if he could get someone to help me get my plane started and on my way. The duty officer had some coffee and rolls handy and offered me some. I accepted his offer and enjoyed a nice big jelly roll.

"Where you headed for, Lieutenant?

"A long way south of here, Captain. About 1500 miles away."

"If you need some coffee to take along, I know we have some thermos jugs in that cabinet." He said as he pointed to a cabinet on the other side of the room.

"Thanks, that sounds like a good idea to me. I walked over and procured a jug and filled it with coffee.

"You can use the black phone if you want to file a flight plan.

I thanked the Captain as I reached for the phone and asked the operator for Air Traffic Control. After talking to them and filing an IFR flight plan, I saw that my help was there to get me started. He offered a good morning and a salute as he told me to let him know when I was ready. I returned the salute and said. "I'm ready now, Sargent."

"I'll pick up a fire extinguisher and meet you at the Mustang. I assume it is the first one in the first line."

I got up, said, "It is," and started to walk out with him.

When we arrived at the plane, I gave it one more check and climbed in. The Sargent was up on the wing to help me strap myself in and hook everything up. He looked at me, "You all set, Lieutenant?"

"I'm all set, Sargent."

"Sir?"

"What is it, Sargent?"

"Good luck."

"Thanks, Sargent, I may need it."

The Sargent offered me another salute and started down to his fire extinguisher. He picked it up and gave me a thumbs up, so I gave the engine a little primer, turned on the mags, and hit the starter. The engine groaned as the prop came to life and started to turn slowly. Fire and smoke jumped out of the exhaust and filled the air. It soon cleared and started to run smoothly. I signaled the Sargent to remove the wheel chocks and added enough throttle to get the plane moving. As I did, I called the tower for taxi instructions. I was directed to runway two-three by the proper taxiways. I looked at my watch and noticed it was 0410, right on time.

I pulled up just short of the runway and turned my plane, so the tail was pointed away from the taxiway. I advanced the throttle and made the necessary engine checks. After I was satisfied all was OK, I called the tower for takeoff clearance. I was cleared onto the duty runway and cleared for takeoff. I pointed the nose down the runway and held my brakes while I advanced the throttle to full open. The engine was running smoothly, so I released my brakes and started my takeoff roll. At first, it started moving slowly, then quickly gained speed as I was flung into the air. I raised my gear, adjusted my throttle and RPM as I started to the heavens. I was already going over 200 knots and still accelerating. I climbed to 10,000 feet and leveled off as I came to the heading of one-seven -five degrees. I again watched as my speed went past 300 knots. When it was where I wanted it, I adjusted the throttle and RPM for cruise. I would stay at 10,000 feet. Above 10,000 feet, I needed oxygen, and I wanted to preserve it. I might need to go higher later on. I was on my way.

I mentally pictured the course I would take. I would fly close to Florida's East coast, widening my distance to it until I was almost abreast of Miami. I would then follow a string of islands, which included the Bahama Islands and Caicos Islands to Haiti on the same course. From there, I would be over open water for the rest of my flight. A distance of fewer than 400 miles. That would be the more risky distance. I should be able to cover it in not much over an hour. My destination was an island called Rutling Island. It was off the coast of Venezuela near Caracas. The total distance was just under 1,500 miles. With a droppable fuel tank, I could get at least 1,600 miles. Some factors would depend on that range. I knew I could take advantage of most of those factors and would.

I called Air Traffic Control and ask for the wind speeds at different altitudes below 10,000 feet. "Roger, Easy five-six-zero, this is Air Traffic Control." My call name was derived from my home base and aircraft serial number. "The best wind is in a Southerly direction at 8,000 feet on a heading of one-eight-five degrees at 60 knots."

"Thanks, Control, change my altitude to 8,000 feet and a heading of one-seven-zero." I wanted a little wind correction so I would fly the correct directions

"Roger, five-six-zero, your cruising altitude is cleared to 8,000 feet at a one-nine-zero degree heading." I settled back for a long trip. The moon was still out, showering me with a rather eerie light. It almost felt like a ghostly light as small clouds, like ghosts, were silhouetted as they passed in front of the moon, only to disappear as new clouds scurried by to replace the one before it.

Below me was a cloudless sky. I could see patches of lights dotting the landscape below me. Some were large, while some were a small solitary group of lights. The large lights marked towns and cities, while the small lights marked individuals. Individuals alone sailing in a black sea of darkness. I could see car lights in strings protruding from the patches of light, especially the large patches. They were like umbilical cords that supplied life to the hungry batches of light.

Occasionally, I could see lights from other airplanes. Some red, some green and some white. Most of the white were flashing and seemed to be saying, "Stay away from me. This is my allotted space in the darkened world we are now in."

As I neared the Eastern coast of Florida, and to amuse myself, I tried to guess which lights marked which city in Florida. As I left the coast and started to fly over the vast expansions of the Atlantic Ocean, the towns seem to disappear and permit only small solitary lights to dot the surface sparsely. Most of the dots were ships. Some were still airplanes that were not forced to cling to the ground as the others were.

Suddenly I was jolted by the radio coming to life. "Easy five-six-zero, this is Air Traffic Control, over." I keyed my mic,

"Roger Air Traffic Control, this is Easy five-six-zero."

"Five-six-zero, you have a large storm with tops to 40,000 feet directly in your path about 100 miles wide. We can guide you around it if you wish."

I hesitated for a couple of minutes. "Control, do you have any reports on how severe it is at 8,000 feet?"

"Five-six-zero, we have one report that it was pretty rough at 12,000 feet."

"Control, I don't have enough fuel to go too far out of my way. Did they report any hail?"

"Just a little, about pea size."

"Control, it may be a little better at 8,000 feet. How about icing?

"Five-six-zero, they had just a little."

"Control, I request permission to go down to 4,000 feet; there should not be icing there.

"Roger, five-six-zero, you are cleared down to 4,000 feet. Good luck."

"Roger, Control, I will keep you informed." I reduced my throttle and started down to 4,000 feet.

After about twenty minutes, I could see a very ominous storm ahead of me. It stretched across the entire horizon as far as I could see. From a distance, I could see most of the storm and how high it was. I am sure it was up to 40,000 feet or more. At the very top, the clouds had formed an anvil head, which would be filled with turbulence. I knew this was an area to be avoided. The turbulence would be extreme and very likely have hail and icing in it. Either of which could be fatal.

I knew if I penetrated the storm at a much lower altitude, I should eliminate the icing. The hail would be another factor to consider.

I tried, in the darkness, to see if there appeared to be a weak spot in its structure. It would almost be impossible to penetrate if I could not find such an entry point. I had a ceiling limit in the P-51 of 42,000 feet if I could get there. It would take a long time to get to that altitude and, even then, the storm may be higher. The top also contains the most violent weather.

I looked again at the storm before me and decided I saw a spot that may show a little less violence. I could handle the turbulence, but the hail would be my nemesis.

As I approached the storm, I slowed the plane down to about 200 knots to lessen the effect of sharp turbulence. I entered the clouds and immediately switched my attention to the instruments in the cockpit. I could barely see my wingtips as the clouds thickened. I could feel the plane bouncing as I entered deeper into the clouds. The turbulence worsened, but I did not see any ice or hailstones.

That continued for over twenty minutes with the plane dropping as much as 200 feet in downdrafts. Now, at times I could hear something hitting my plane. I knew this was hail, but I was too busy flying on instruments to look out. At times, the surrounding clouds would grow lighter, and the turbulence would lesson only to, again, grow darker with the rain, hail, and turbulence increasing. The turbulence became so bad at times that the plane would just be rocked from side to side as it caught a downdraft and plunged downward for 300 feet or more. A couple of times, the turbulence became so bad it would almost turn the plane to an inverted attitude.

After about the first twenty minutes, the clouds became lighter, and the turbulence and precipitation lessened. I finally broke out into a world filled with sunshine. It almost felt like I had just stepped out of a dark closet into a well-lit room. I must say it was very welcome.

I quickly visually checked the outside surface of the plane to see if there was any damage from the hail. With the low light, it was difficult to tell. I thought I might see some small dents in the leading edge of my wings, but I was not sure. The plane was flying well, and that is what counted. I called, and received, permission from Air Traffic Control to climb back to 8,000 feet. I advanced my throttle to start that climb and return to my cruising airspeed.

I wondered if the storm had thrown me off-course. I began to crank in some different radio stations to find out. If I knew who they were and where they were, I could get a good position from where they intersected. I may have been a little off course, so I adjusted my heading to the necessary corrections.

I determined I was still over some islands and about a quarter of the way to my destination. I still had a long way to go. Might as well sit back and relax.

I was kept busy with my navigating to make sure I stayed on the right course. At certain points, I would have to check in with Air Traffic Control, so they knew I was on the right track. I could still see a lot of small islands passing under me. I was still about an hour and a half from Haiti and would be near the Caicos Islands.

I decided to have some coffee to help the time pass. I had shoved the thermos bottle into one of my flight suit pockets, which was now a little difficult to get out. As I was doing battle with my thermos, the radio came to life. "Five-six-zero, this is Air Traffic Control, over."

"Air Traffic Control, this is five-six-zero."

"Five-six-zero, the winds have changed. The wind has come around to the South and is now in your face at forty-five knots. You have a better wind at 1,4000 feet in the direction of one-nine-five degrees at thirty-five knots."

"Control, what are they at 10,000 feet?"

"Five-six-zero, they, are in the direction of one-eight-zero degrees at thirty Knots."

"Control, request altitude change to 10,000 feet."

"Five-six-zero, you are cleared to climb to 10,000 feet."

"Roger Control, climbing to 10,000 feet."

At 10,000 feet, I could still leave my oxygen mask off. At 10,000 feet. I could also still enjoy my coffee.

I could now see Haiti coming up. I was right on course and about two hours from my destination. After the storm, it had turned into a beautiful day, with the sun dominating a cloudless sky. I thought for a moment. I could see the Sun smiling. I would wait for another hour and try to contact my island.

As I passed over Haiti, I bid the land goodbye and started my lonely trek over a vast ocean. I would not see land again for close to two hours. It kind of reminded me that we, as Navy pilots, spent much of our time over water. It was nothing new, but it still gave me a rather isolated feeling.

I knew I was getting close when I passed near Aruba. I was not sure I would be able to see Aruba, but there it was. A beautiful little island, maybe it was just a dot in a vast ocean. I did not think I would be close enough to see Aruba, but, again, there it was. I was getting close to my destination, so I decided just to sit back and enjoy the scenery.

CHAPTER VI

I continued on for a short time and decided to give Rutling a call. Before I could key the mic, the radio exploded into life with people yelling in Spanish. I had no idea what they were saying, but I knew something was going down that was creating a panic situation. It continued for several minutes, followed by a lull. I decided to ask someone what was going on.

"This is five-six-zero, I am in your vicinity, can I be of assistance to you?"

"Five-six-zero, this is Rutling, we have one of our planes under hostile actions about fifty miles from us. Can you help?"

"Rutling, have them give me a long count so I can get a bearing on them."

Rutling never answered; instead, I heard a very excited voice start to count. I am sure he was overly excited since he was counting in Spanish.

"Whoever is counting in Spanish, I have a bearing on you; in fact, I think I can see you. I see several planes, are you more than one plane?"

I was already turning in that direction, donning my oxygen mask, and starting to climb.

I heard a rapid flow of Spanish follow.

I broke in and repeatedly said, "English, English, please."

I heard back, "We are one plane and have two planes attacking us. They have fired their guns."

I was coming up behind them, so they did not see me. I saw two German ME-109s on each side of a twin-engine civilian plane, and two more ME-109s higher and out to the right. Without hesitation, I armed all six of my machine guns. I could see the two planes beside the twin-engine were trying to get them to change direction toward the mainland. They were sporadically firing their machine guns.

"This is five-six-zero, what's the situation?" I did not want to tell him I was behind him since I thought the ME-109s might be on this frequency.

"We are being attacked. They are shooting at us. Can you help?"

"Who are you?"

"We have the president of Rutling and his family with us."

I didn't need to hear anymore. I knew all the ME-109 pilots were too busy doing what they were doing to look around for another plane. I decided the ME-109s were too close to the twin-engine for me to take a shot at them. I may hit the twin-engine. I also knew that if I did shoot at the ME-109s by the twin-engine, the other two could be on me in an instant and shoot me down. I had only one choice, which was to take the two highest ME-109s first. If I could get both of them, I could then go after the other two beside the twin-engine.

The only thing that could go wrong was for the two beside the plane to drop back and shoot at the twin-engine. I did not think they would have time. First, it would be a total surprise to them, and they would take precious seconds to figure it out before they could act.

I slowly came up behind the two high ME-109s so as not to alert any of the planes. I stayed back far enough to avoid any debris that would come off the ME-109s. I dropped my external fuel tank to give me more maneuverability and opened fire on the left ME-109. Almost at the same time, I kicked my nose around to my right without letting up on the trigger. The left had his right wing fail about halfway up and break off the plane. He was already bailing out. The other ME-109 immediately started to belch white smoke. I didn't have time to stay any longer. I knew he was out of the fight, so I left him.

As I pushed my nose down toward the other two, I could see that I had startled them enough to make them lose their concentration on the twin-engine. Both relaxed their positions, dropping below and behind the twin-engine, giving me a clear shot at the one on the right. It only took me seconds to get into position and fire at him. As I fired, I saw his landing gear drop, followed by a small trail of black smoke erupting from the underside of the motor. I knew I had hit him hard to make the gear drop, but I didn't have time to stay with him. I had another ME-109 to deal with. I didn't want him to turn around and come back. I had to put him out of action too.

The last ME-109 must have thought he didn't want any part of all this and decided to hightail it for home, but I wasn't sure. As he dove away, I fell in behind him. He was too far away to shoot at, but I knew I had a faster plane. I pushed the throttle to fully open and went after him. He knew I was closing on him, so he made a sharp bank to the right and closed his throttle to make me overshoot and let him get a shot at me.

I think I had to be grinning when I said to myself. "Friend, you're doing that to the wrong guy." I had seen this in combat over France. The German pilots used this trick when they knew you had them, and they couldn't outrun you. When they chopped their throttle and broke right, it would take you a few seconds to do the same, which would make you overrun them. All they had to do was to go to full throttle, brake back left, fall in behind you since they knew you would chop your throttle in response and slow down. It was then simple to line up on the p-51 and pull the trigger.

This time, I also chopped my throttle, did a barrel roll, kind of a sideways loop, to the left to use up my extra speed, and slid right back in behind him as I rolled out of my barrel roll. He would be looking for me ahead of him, but I was right behind him. The rest was simple. Squeeze the trigger. As I did, debris from his wing almost hit my plane. I knew he was out of the fight and would have trouble just getting home, so I broke it off.

I caught the twin-engine plane on its way to Rutling and joined up with it. The pilot on the left was waving at me and kept giving me a thumbs up. I could see several other people glued to their window. As we reached the airfield, the twin-engine plane made a straight-in approach to the runway while I held my altitude and went into a regular break and landing.

The twin-engine plane was directed into a waiting hanger. I was directed into a different hanger some distance away.

As I departed from my plane, I was met by a man who appeared to be a different nationality then South American. "Welcome to Rutling. I hope you had a nice trip."

"Thank you, I did indeed, although it was a little exciting at times."

"I am sure it was we were listening to the radio and caught it all. You have only been here a short time, and already you are a hero."

"That remains to be seen, but thank you."

I think he must have noticed my name on my flight suit. "Lieutenant, you are to wait here for a car to pick you up."

"Thank you."

When the car arrived, I stepped in and asked the driver where we were going.

"I am to take you to President Villa's residence."

That seemed to end the conversation, so I just sat back and relaxed. We arrived at our destination rather quickly. I departed the car and walked up to the entrance.

After a knock on the door, someone came to answer it. "How may I help you, Sir?" It was a well-dressed gentleman who I assumed was some sort of butler or assistant.

"I am Lieutenant Baker to see the president."

"Come in, Sir. Please follow me." I followed the man as he led me to a study and told me that the president would be there shortly. There was a large desk at one end with a large table and chairs a short distance away. Several lounge chairs also occupied the room. I walked in and seated myself in one of the lounge chairs close to the desk. I did not have to wait long before President Villa entered the room, accompanied by two other gentlemen. "Good morning, Lieutenant, I need to first thank you for what you did today. I am quite certain I would not be here if you had not intervened. That was a remarkable display of courage and ability. I was impressed beyond my ability to tell you. Thank you again."

"Thank you, Mr. President, I am pleased I could be of service to you."

"It was certainly more than just a service, Lieutenant. You potentially saved my life as well as that of my family. I will be forever in your debt. How long will you be able to stay with us, Lieutenant?"

"I am due back to my squadron Wednesday, so I will need to leave in the morning."

"I wish you could stay longer. Is there anything I can do to facilitate that?"

"That is up to my commanding officer, sir."

The president turned to one of the gentlemen with him and told him to make a note of that. He then asked me, "What is your squadron, Lieutenant?"

"It is VF-21 in Jacksonville, Florida, Sir."

"Did you have a good trip down, Lieutenant?"

"Not too bad, Sir. I encountered a massive storm North of Haiti. It was a little rough going through."

"Were you aware of our situation when you first contacted us?"

"It did not take long to see that someone was trying to divert you to another destination. I presumed they would not stop at anything to make that happen. That would include shooting your airplane down. I did not want to use excessive force, but I knew I had to take whatever action was necessary, so I did."

"That is exactly right. I have no doubt they would have resorted to that if we did not do as they wanted us to. I feel confident that you saved the life of everyone on our plane. I am especially grateful for you saving my family. Thank you again, Lieutenant."

I just nodded my recognition.

The President continued. "This could very well turn into a very grave situation. The opposition will undoubtedly try to turn this around to make it a hostile action on our part. They will portray us as the aggressor and try to convince everyone that we are very hostile."

"How could they do that, Sir, you were in an unarmed plane. They had surrounded you and were trying to divert you to a different destination?"

"I know that is true, but no one was there to substantiate that. Only you and they will say we hired you to say that."

"I was not yet working for you, Sir. I had only come down to see if I wanted to. I had not made any commitments and will state that I would not work for a hostile country. I only wanted to be an advisor, Sir. I was to advise you on your Air Force, and that is entirely true.

I have had enough combat and do not want to see anymore."

"I am afraid they will also accuse the United States of having you doing their bidding."

"Sir, I am due to be released from active duty in four weeks. I was not on any service-connected mission."

"We will try to avoid that situation if at all possible, Lieutenant. I am still very thankful that you did show up when you did."

One of the gentlemen had left the room earlier while we were talking. He had just stepped into the room. "Mr. President, we have permission for Lieutenant Baker to be back at his duty station on Monday, a week from today."

The President thanked him and turned in my direction. "I hope you will be our guest until that time, Lieutenant."

"I guess I don't have to be anywhere else, Sir. I will leave that up to you."

The gentleman that just returned interrupted. "They have also instructed the Lieutenant to return by their transportation. They will have a plane pick him up on Saturday or Sunday. He is to leave the P-51 that he delivered to us here and deliver another one at a later date. He is also to avoid any further unnecessary contact with the hostile party."

"Thank you, Ed. The President looked at me. I think you will be our guest for the next few days, Lieutenant, I will be looking forward to your stay. We can cover a lot of ground, and I do want my family to meet you. I am sure they will want to thank you personally."

"Mr. President, I have only brought my flight suit along. I am afraid I also left my money at home as well.

Can you contact my squadron and request a loan of sorts? I will need some clothing and possibly other essentials. Unless, of course, it is permissible for me to wear a flight suit. I can do that, but I may need some other essential clothing and a frequent laundry facility."

"Lieutenant, you will have little need for money here. I will send someone over to see that you have everything you will need."

The President started to leave, stopped, and said. "I hope you will dine with my family and myself this evening. I will have a very reliable person to guide you around. Thank you again. I will look forward to seeing you about six this evening, Lieutenant."

I stood there a little bewildered, trying to digest all that had gone on. Someone entered the room, offered me something to drink and eat, and told me to be comfortable. Someone would be with me within the hour.

I accepted the offer of a drink and light snack since it had been a long time since I had last eaten. I sat down and waited. In a few minutes, someone brought me some refreshments and, again, told me it could be an hour or so before someone would call for me. I thanked them.

It had been a long time since I had last slept, so I finished my snack and sat down to relax. I wondered what I had gotten myself in for. That was the last I remember. I was awakened by a feminine voice, softly repeating, "Lieutenant, Lieutenant." I slowly came back to reality and observed the world through a very foggy haze. I looked up and saw a young lady standing over me. It still took me a short time to come back to full reality. When I did look directly at her, I saw a radiant smile and heard a pleasant voice say. "I am Mia. I am to take you around and get you what you need." I still sat there a little stunned, wondering who this angel was that came to greet me.

I sat up, "Mia, you startled me. I thought I was in heaven seeing an angel. I may not be in heaven, but I think I am still seeing an angel."

"I am certainly not an angel, but thank you for the thought. I was told you need some clothing and other essentials. I will be at your service. Tell me what you need, and I will take you where you can get it."

"I hope you have some money. I am afraid I left everything back in the States."

"I have an open account; I am to get you whatever you need. Just tell me what you want."

"That is a very open account. Is it reserved for material things?"

"What do you mean, Lieutenant."

"First of all, I am tired of being called Lieutenant. My name is Bob, and I wish you would call me that. Is that on your list?"

"If it isn't, Bob, I will see that it is added."

"Thank you, Mia, I think we are off to an excellent start. Secondly, I have not had a friendly hug for a very long time. Do you have a friendly hug on your list? Nothing romantic, just a friendly hug like my Mother used to give me."

"Bob, I know that kind of a hug very well. I will certainly give you one and ask my Mother to give you one later." I then receive a very Motherly hug.

"Thank you, Mia, that was very sweet of you. I am not trying to be forward or make advances. I am honestly a hugger and feel that is the best way to tell someone you like them, and I like you. You are a very delightful young lady. Thank you, I now pronounce us friends."

"You know something, Bob? I do feel like I have known you for a long time, and we are friends.

"See what I mean, Mia? I think we will have a much more enjoyable day now."

"I know we will, Bob. I don't think your day had a very enjoyable start with what you did earlier."

"Mia, I never like to start or end a day with taking someone's life. I don't think I did today and hope I didn't. I hope every one of the pilots I shot down today survived. I think they did. I tried to let them live. It can be tough to live with otherwise."

"Bob, you shot down four airplanes, how can you avoid not killing them?"

"It was not easy, but I think I did. I did not shoot all of the planes down. Only two and those two both bailed out. I stopped firing when I could, so I would give them time to get out of their plane. I saw both chutes open. One of the others, I shot low to avoid the cockpit and hit his underside. The gear broke loose and dropped down. He had a little black smoke from the underside of his engine. He had a chance of making it home or bailing out. The last had run away from the fight, but I thought he might turn back and catch both of our planes when we were at a disadvantage. He pulled a great maneuver that could have gotten me, but I knew what it was. I managed to hit him in his wing area and saw debris come off. I avoided the cockpit. I did a lot of damage to him, which I am sure I convinced him to go home in a damaged plane that he would have trouble fighting in."

"Bob, that is remarkable; it is hard for me to understand how someone could have that kind of compassion."

"I could have killed most or all, and maybe I should have. All of them now have the chance to kill me if we meet again."

"Bob, I hope we can settle this and stop this situation before it goes to something worse. I am tired of being under the stress our country is in."

"I hope that will be possible, Mia."

"Why are you here helping us, Bob, if you feel that way?

"After today, I have started to wonder that myself. I did commit, Mia. Maybe I can make a difference. Perhaps I can help save lives instead of taking them."

I could see a tear in the corner of Mia's eye. She grabbed me and gave me a long and firm hug. "Who are you, Bob? Where did you come from? You can't be human. Are you some sort of an Angel?"

"I am certainly not an angel, Mia. Come on. Let's go and find me some new socks. Mia, I think I made a friend today. See what just one hug can do?"

"It may have started with a simple hug, Bob, but it is something much more now than just friends. You are at the top of that list and started another of the people I would like in my life."

"I am touched, Mia. That will certainly at least be for the next six or seven days, I hope."

We walked out to Mia's car hand in hand. I knew I had made a lifelong friend.

We did visit several shops in a lovely city. I purchased a suit and tie, a couple of pairs of trousers, and several shirts. I also included some socks, but I made Mia turn her head when I found some underwear. She giggled and just squeezed my hand she was holding. Mia was very quick to advise me on the appropriate style I should choose. She said she didn't want me to look funny while I was with her.

"Mia, I hope that is a thought you would like to see me again, or is that merely an assumption on my part."

"How would you like it to be, Bob?

"Can you give me a list to choose from, or must I simply ad-lib my choice?"

"Let me think about that for a while. Mia put her finger under her chin as if deep in thought. We continued walking while she kept her finger under her chin and rocking her head from side to side."

"I'm getting worried, Mia. You are taking too long making that decision. I may have to intervene."

"I'm still thinking, Bob. I need more time."

"Mia, your time is up. I am going to accept it as if you want to see me again. You no longer have a choice. You are stuck with me for the next few days. Like it or not."

Mia stopped and looked at me with a solemn look. A smile started to creep across her face. "I like it very much, Bob. Mia drove me home, where we separated with a hug. I went into my quarters to rest before the evening events.

CHAPTER VII

About 1700 hours, I received a call from Mia, telling me she would pick me up about 1730 to take me to the President's dinner. I asked. "Will you be at the dinner, Mia?"

"Yes, I will, Bob."

"Wow, I will be riding with a very important woman."

"I don't know how important I am, but I will be there."

"Mia, I am happy you will be there. I hope you will get me out of trouble if I say or do the wrong thing. Can I depend on that?

"You can, Bob. Is that the only reason you would like me to be there?"

"I would be lying if I said otherwise, Mia. I think you know how much I enjoyed the time we spent together today."

"We can discuss that later, Bob. I will see you at 5:30. Goodbye."

I finished dressing and sat down to wait for Mia.

Mia was there to pick me up right on time. As I opened the car door and greeted her, I noticed she had on an evening gown. It was gorgeous, and so was she. "Mia, you are absolutely stunning. You have taken my breath away and left me speechless. I think you are the prettiest girl I have ever seen."

"Thank you, Bob. I bet you tell that to all the girls you date.

"I have not dated a lot because of the war, but the answer to what you have said is no."

"I think you are kidding me, Bob. I am sure you have a date every night."

"I never did find any girls on the carrier. Before I returned, I was a German prisoner for seven months. There sure weren't any girls in the prison camp. I also did not want to get serious with anyone because of what I was doing. I didn't want a wife left crying back home with children to raise alone."

"Didn't you have a girlfriend back home when you joined the Navy?"

"I did, but that didn't last long when I was gone so much and felt the way I did."

"Do you still feel that way, Bob?

"I haven't had a chance to find out. I just got out of the prison camp not long ago. If I would have stayed in the Navy and been settled down, I think I would like to have someone in my life. I am 28 now and still unsettled. I'm afraid I may never be able to follow that dream. How about you, Mia?"

"My story is a little different. Oops, we are here. I would love to finish this conversation later. Promise me we will?"

"I want to hear your story. It is definitely a promise."

As we pulled up in the drive to our entrance, we were met by a parking assistant who helped Mia out of her car and said something in Spanish. My door was also opened for me. I walked around the car, where I met Mia. Mia offered me her hand, which I took as we walked together toward the entrance.

"Mia, I feel a little out of place. Everyone is in formal dress. Will they make me eat in the kitchen by myself?"

"If they do, I will eat with you. I don't think you need to be concerned. You are the guest of honor."

I just stopped short. No one told me that. The other guests may laugh at the way I am dressed. Let's go home."

"Have no fear, Bob. I will protect you. Now stand tall and walk in like a man."

"Do I have a choice?"

"No."

"OK, Skipper, lead the way, and I will follow."

"That's a good boy, just do as I tell you."

We walked across the floor to where the President was standing with a woman. I presumed she was his wife.

President Villa reached out, shook my hand, and welcomed me to the dinner. Mia then turned to the lady and said, I would also like you to meet Carman, President Villa's wife."

"I have been looking forward to meeting you, Mrs. Villa, I am looking forward to meeting your daughter as well."

"I think you already have, Lieutenant."

I know I had a surprised look on my face as I murmured, "I don't think I have."

Mia took over the conversation. "Bob likes motherly hugs. I told him I would have my mother hug him. Mom, would you hug Bob, so he feels more at home with us?"

I was utterly paralyzed and speechless as Carman stepped over and put her arms around my neck. "I also like to give nice young men a kiss on the cheek for saving my life." I did receive both a hug and a kiss on the cheek. I returned the hug and said.

"And I like to give a hug and kiss to all the ladies whose lives I have saved. I kissed her on her cheek in return." I just stepped back and looked at Mia. "Paybacks are fun, Mia."

I heard a big round of applause come from the folks who now surrounded us.

President Villa asked everyone to be seated and announced that cocktails would be continued while he said a few things. I was surprised that he was speaking in English. He gave an introduction to me and said what I had done. He continued with my service in the US Navy and that he hoped I would stay and continue to aid his and their country. It was a very eloquent speech followed by asking me to say a few words.

I arose. "President Villa, Mrs. Villa, Mia, and guests, I am not a soldier of fortune nor a person who likes war, fighting, and death. If you are looking for that person, you will not find him standing here. When I was first told you needed pilots here, I had a very thirsty desire to continue flying. I knew that could include many dangers, including death. I am no longer that man. I will not accept your offer for that reason. I have had a lot of time to think about all this on my five-hour trip down here. I did engage in hostile aircraft intent on killing your president and his family. I felt, all at once, I didn't want to kill anyone, but I knew I had to do something. I did go into battle with the primary thought of doing what I had to do to save the people in that airplane, even kill."

"I did something I had never done before. I tried to shoot down those planes without killing the pilots. I think I accomplished that, and I feel good about it."

"I met three of the most outstanding people in my life when I arrived here. I now understand what they feel, what they think, and what they want. I was beginning to think I would turn down your offer and go back home. I can't do that now. Your cause is real, your cause is justified, and your cause is noble. If there is a chance to achieve it, I think it can be achieved without bloodshed. I would advocate that avenue, if at all possible. If it cannot be, I now have a reason to help, and I will help. That reason is the people of this island. I don't know why, and yet I do know why. Mia has shown me who you are and what you want. The time I spent with her today is a time that will live with me forever. I have never met nicer people. However, I must admit that Mia is a little devious. I spent most of the day with her, and she never told me she was President Villa's daughter. I think I can find it in my heart to forgive her, but it may take a while. I hope I am allowed that time." I looked at Mia and saw her shaking her head, yes.

The dinner and the small talk went well. As we parted, President Villa told me he was very pleased with what I had said and asked me to call his office in the morning to set up a time for a meeting. I assured him I would. There were a lot of handshakes on the way out, but Mia and I managed to escape to her car. As Mia drove me back to my quarters, I asked her to tell me more about her life. Our conversation had been cut short on the way to the dinner.

"Bob, do you really want to know about my life? It may not be that interesting."

"Mia, any part of your life, holds my interest. I want to know as much as I can about you, and as much as you care to share with me."

"There is not much to tell, Bob. I am 24 now. I graduated from college two years ago with a degree in business. Dad and I thought it would be most beneficial if I would be involved in helping him. I dated a lot when I was in college, but have not so much since. I did have a steady boyfriend for a few months after I came home from college, but I just date once in a while now. I think men are afraid of me because of my father. I guess that is where I am now. I told you it would not be too thrilling. Certainly not like yours."

"Believe me, Mia, yours is much saner than mine. I would rather live a life you just described than the one I have had. I am in a rut and can't get out."

"You can get out of it, Bob. Make the decision and do it."

"I don't know what I would do. This is all I have ever done, the only thing I am good at, but good will end someday, one way or the other."

"Don't say that, Bob."

"I will admit, meeting you has made me pause and think about it."

We arrived at my quarters, which seemed to end the conversation.

"Mia, I would ask you in, but I don't have much here to offer you unless you enjoy looking at an empty room."

"That would not be a problem with you there, but I don't think it would look good. May I take a rain check?"

"That is now an open invitation. Mia, I can't tell you how much I have enjoyed meeting you. It has been a highlight in my life."

I opened the car door and started to get out.

"Bob, I would like to see you again. I know we will with what is happening, but I mean." Mia hesitated. "You know what I mean."

Now it was my turn to hesitate. "Mia, I was trying to find a way to ask if I could see you again, but I didn't know if I should."

"Why wouldn't you,"

"I may not be here that long. I know I would get to like you too much and then have to leave. Would you consider a real date and take the risk?"

"Is that just a question, or are you asking?"

"Mia, I'm not asking, I am begging."

Mia slid over closer, took hold of my suit labels, and gave me a gentle kiss. "Is that a good enough answer?"

I opened my car door, walked around to her side, opened her door, and pulled her close as she stood up. I gave her a very warm and passionate kiss and said. "I like the way you answer questions."

Mia put her arms around my neck and kissed me. I shall never forget it. "Bob, I just want to make sure you understood my answer."

"I think I have your answer. Call me in the morning. I will need a ride to see your father." We bid each other good night and parted.

The next morning, Mia called about 0800 and told me she would pick me up so we could have breakfast together. She told me her father was having an important meeting that he wanted me to be at. I thanked Mia and waited for her to arrive.

We enjoyed a delightful breakfast and decided to go out later this evening on an official date. I think we were both anxious. I told Mia to plan where we would go and reminded her that I did not have any money. She said she had talked to her father about that and he would give me an advance.

After breakfast, and a pleasant conversation with Mia, I started to the room President Villa wood hold the meeting in. As I walked in, President Villa greeted me with a handshake and introduced me to the others who were present in the room. Most were cabinet members or advisers.

Everyone was talking in English, which I thought rather odd. I asked President Villa why they were not speaking in Spanish. President Villa smiled and said. "Lieutenant, we are kind of an exception to the rule for this part of the world. This Island was settled by the British many years ago. They, of course, introduced English. Since most of the countries down here speak Spanish, we have become a bilingual country. We still use English, but many here also use Spanish, so both are spoken."

"I never knew that, thank you."

President Villa went on. "We have some significant changes and a situation to address this morning. Most of it concerns you. As I told you, our opposition has complained to Venezuela and the US about what took place. They know you are from the US and still in the Navy. Venezuela has said that the incident, the one you were in, occurred over international waters, so they have no control over it. The US has maintained that you were delivering a plane to Rutling and was drawn into the conflict to help President Villa, who was in a distressed situation. They justified your intervention was prompted by your desire to aid a country friendly to the US. The planes were German, which was confusing since Germany had surrendered and was to cease all hostilities. Any aggression by forces of Germany would be considered an act of war and dealt with as such. The US reserved the right to eliminate such forces if they were a threat, no matter where they were located."

"The US will contact you, stating that you have been designated an advisor to Rutling, and your release from active duty is being extended. You will also receive a promotion to that of a Lieutenant Commander. A representative from your Navy will be here to brief you on your new duties."

"Wow, Mr. President, I never expected anything like this."

"Commander, I have taken the liberty to have new uniforms tailored for you. I have the first one here so you can wear it today. We will finish tailoring it and do the others after this meeting. Mia has your uniform and will help you with it in case it needs further work now. Return here after you have it, and we will continue your briefing."

"Yes, Sir. I will be back as soon as I can."

I left the room and found Mia in the hall. "I didn't know, I would see you so soon. Where do we go?"

"A tailor was waiting for us in a nearby room to help me if I needed more fitting.

"I didn't know this was going to happen, Bob, or I would have told you."

"I know you would have, Mia. I am still wondering what is happening. I hope our date for later is still on."

"It is, Bob. Now I will leave you to your fitting. I will talk to you later." She stepped out of the room and was gone.

The uniform fit well with only a few minor alterations to be done later. I thanked the tailor and started back to the meeting room.

As I returned to the meeting room, the President saw me right away and came over. "That didn't take long. How does it fit?"

"Perfect, how did you know my size?"

"Mia was with you when you purchased your clothes the other day. She guessed the rest. I am going to turn you over to Jose. He will finish the briefing and school you on what to expect."

I was immediately handed over to Jose, who started to bring me up to date. We would meet with the opposition soon.

"Commander, I will tell you what we know, the format we would like you to follow, and what to expect. We know that one of the senior members of the hostiles will be there along with a couple of his top men. We also know the four pilots you dealt with will accompany them and be questioned."

"You can expect them all to state that you initiated the attack and was the aggressive one. The pilots will say that they were only checking the plane out and did not intend to harm anyone. We would like you to play along with them, but not admitting any wrongdoing. They have been informed that you did not shoot to kill, so I know they will question that."

"We have a big surprise for them. Pictures were taken from our plane, showing them firing their guns when they were alongside. Don't give this away. We will surprise them with it. We want you to say that you were coming down to assess the situation and deliver a plane."

"Jose, I will not lie about anything under any circumstances. If asked, I will say that I flew down in one of Rutling's planes to assess the situation. This is the truth. If they asked if I was delivering it, I would tell them. I could leave it here or fly it back. I would do as ordered."

"Please cooperate with us, Commander.

Lying is not cooperating; it is being dishonest. I have not felt the need to do that. If I have an honest question, I will give an honest answer. We are in the right. If I tell even a small lie and it is detected, it will discredit everything I have said."

President Villa happened to be listening to what I said. Jose was looking at him as if to seek an answer.

"Commander, I have never heard a better reason for being honest. You have taught us a fundamental lesson in honesty. We have nothing to hide, and you are right. Commander, if even a small untruth is detected, it will discredit all the truths you have given."

That is the way I am, Sir. I value my integrity.

Jose covered a few more minor points, shook hands, and departed.

The meeting was to take place on a nearby mutual island a short distance away. It was to start at 1300 hours, and it was now 1100 hours. Since it was so close, the President decided to take a yacht that Rutling owned. We would have lunch on the way over. The rest, including the Navy representative, would fly in. I saw Mia before we left and told her I did not know when we would get back. She just said she wanted to spend some time with me anyway. I readily agreed.

Everyone arrived, and the meeting started on time. The Navy Representative was Captain Jones. I spoke with him briefly and helped fill him in on some things he should know. The captain reaffirmed my retention on active duty and promotion to Lieutenant Commander.

We were all seated around a massive table, with each group seated together. We had three moderators from other countries that would oversee the meeting and ensure a proper representation from all involved.

It began with the German organization that had filed the complaint. Their representative, when questioned by the moderators, stated that they had a flight of four ME-109s on a routine training mission when they saw the twin-engine plane, they flew over to it to make an identification. They just wanted to know who it was and if it could be having difficulty. Two of the pilots did join up on it to determine if it was in trouble and to make a positive identification. They went on to say that while they were there, a P-51 from Rutling attacked, first the two higher ME-109s and then the lower two. They described that I took a relentless approach to destroy their airplanes and kill the pilots. One of the pilots described how I stayed behind him and continued shooting until I thought he was dead. Only one described my action as a fair fight with him. He was a Major. I immediately had respect for him. He was the last one I had encountered. The question was also brought up as to why I was armed for a ferry flight.

I was next. "Commander Baker, we have heard from the party making the complaint. We would like to now hear from you, in your own words, what took place."

"Thank you. It was quite a bit different than the version given to you a few minutes ago. I was on my way to Rutling to evaluate the situation that existed between Rutling and a group flying Me-109s. It was this group that I encountered. I was told they were trying to take over Rutling Island to use for themselves. Rutling needed an advisor to help them defend themselves. Since I had a lot of experience, I was asked and volunteered to visit them to assess the situation and see if I would help them. I had not decided one way or the other at that time. I did feel that they may need help because of their inexperience. I was permitted to use one of their P-51s to fly down and visit them. I had been told the other party had demonstrated hostile acts. As a precaution to protect myself, I had my guns armed. That is the only reason. I would not initiate any action, but I was prepared, if it became necessary, to defend myself."

"As I was coming into the vicinity of Rutling, I heard an animated exchange of words in Spanish. I do not understand Spanish, but I do understand when someone is in trouble regardless of the language. When the talking subsided, I put out a call to see if I could be of assistance. A call from Rutling informed me of what was going on. The pilot of the plane being attacked screamed that they were being attacked and that they had been fired on. I asked them to identify themselves, which they did. I caught sight of them some distance away. I immediately turned in that direction. As I approached, I could see that two ME-109s were in tight formation with the twin-engine and sporadically firing their guns. It appeared as an attempt to make them change directions. There were also two ME-109s high and to the right."

"I knew I was no match for four ME-109s unless I had the advantage of surprise. I knew I had to put the top two out of commission, or they would get me. I came up behind them and fired at the one on the left, aiming for his left wing to avoid killing the pilot. The wing did separate about halfway up, so I continued on to the one on the right and fired low to miss the pilot. As soon as I saw black smoke, I stopped firing."

"I moved to the other two. I fired low at the one on the right. I saw his gear go down and white smoke. I knew I had not hit the pilot. The last one was diving away, so I followed. When I was able, I fired mostly at his left wing. I knew I hit the plane, so I broke it off. I thought he would keep going since his plane was damaged. That is the way it was. I did not have a desire to kill anyone. I could have easily killed all of you." I pointed to each German Pilot. "I didn't have the stomach for it. I did shoot down seven planes while I was in combat, but something changed me. It was a German officer that caused that change."

I stopped for a few seconds. I was a prisoner in a German prison camp in France. A German officer by the name of Fred saved my life more than once when prisoners were taken out and shot because there were too many of them. Fred was taking a large group of prisoners back to the rear to save our lives. As I stood beside him, he was shot by a 17-year-old French girl who did not know what Fred was doing. He died in my arms. I was dampened by his blood as I held him and watched him die. I think I spared you because of Fred."

I sat down. No one spoke, and no one moved for several minutes. Finally, one of the moderators broke the silence. "Thank you, Commander. I will allow questions at this time." The German major raised his hand and was acknowledged.

"Commander, you know the best way would have been to kill us and eliminate the possibility of dealing with us again. That is the part I don't understand."

"Major, you are correct, and that is the practical way. We can eliminate the possibility of us meeting again here today if we will only understand each other and work together. We have that opportunity now if we will work together. That possibility has been laid at our doorstep, let us pick it up and acknowledged this opportunity. I look forward to meeting you again, Major, but not in the sky. I would like it to be over a cup of coffee as friends."

"Thank you, Commander, I too would welcome that day." The room again fell silent, then continued with a few more questions.

We were informed by one of the moderators that Venezuela had declined to come to this meeting. They had sent a message saying that this incident took place over international waters, and they had no control over it.

When the representative from Rutling was interviewed, they produced a picture of one of the ME-109s alongside their plane firing its guns. The German representative jumped to claim it as a stock picture, and the event did not occur when they were checking the aircraft from Rutling. He struck his fist on the table and said. "If Rutling is going to use lies and deception, this meeting is over." He gathered his papers and stormed out of the room, followed by the rest of his group. Only one remained. It was the Major.

The senior moderator declared the meeting closed. The meeting was over, along with an opportunity that may not come again. The German Major stood up, looked at me, and saluted. I returned the salute.

On the way out of the building, President Villa informed me he had expedited having the new pilots report in. He had done that yesterday in anticipation of things not going well at this meeting. He explained that if things didn't go well, we might experience some aggression on their part. They would be here very soon.

CHAPTER VIII

The trip back to Rutling was somber, an expression of our disappointment. Captain Jones from the US Navy accompanied us back to Rutling. He did offer some hope that the US could put some pressure on the necessary parties to get their attention, as he put it. I asked him what he wanted me to do. "Commander Baker, we are in a state of limbo, just keep a low profile and avoid any contact with the hostile party. I will consult with Admiral Dean and get back to you."

I was anxious to get back and talk to Mia. I knew I would have to hold Captain Jones's hand while he was here and would not be able to keep our date. I hoped her father would include Mia in whatever we did.

President Villa did invite Captain Jones to have dinner with him. I, of course, would have to attend. I knew Mia would not be there since this would be considered a business meeting of sorts.

I found Mia when we arrived back in Rutling and informed her that I would be expected to spend the evening with her father and Captain Jones. I did receive a warm hug from Mia, accompanied by a disappointing look. We decided, if I was able to break away and it was not late, we would spend a little time together.

Captain Jones was taken to, what would be his quarters for the night, to freshen up and return for cocktails and dinner. President Villa had a car assigned to me, so I would have more freedom and not find it necessary to rely on Mia.

When I arrived back, Captain Jones was already there, so I joined them in a sitting room. I had hoped Mia and her mother would be present, but I was disappointed as I knew I would be. The conversation was centered on the happenings of the day and what choices we had in the near future. President Villa had invited others to the dinner, mostly those who had an interest in what was currently taking place. The dinner was void of the current situation and centered on our guest of honor, who was Captain Jones.

President Villa, Captain Jones, and I would meet for breakfast, followed by a meeting that would just be the three of us. We had to map out plans to present to Admiral Dean.

I was able to talk to Mia for a short time. We made plans to meet after the meeting with Captain Jones and spend as much of the day together as we could. We would have dinner out and just enjoy each other's company.

While we were still in the meeting with Captain Jones, President Villa received a call that radar had picked up aircraft in the vicinity of Rutling. As soon as President Villa received the call, I started for the airfield. I asked President Villa to call ahead and tell them to have my plane fully armed and ready. I shook hands with Captain Jones and departed.

I had my flight gear in the plane. All I had to do was put it on and get in the plane. I had not noticed my lineman, but I heard someone say. "Good luck, Lieutenant." I then noticed it was the same man that had welcomed me when I first arrived.

"Thank you, what is your name?"

"Pete. Sir."

"Pete, you are from now on, my plane captain. It's Lieutenant Commander now."

As he was helping me get ready, he said. "Good luck, Commander."

"Thanks, Pete, say a prayer for me."

"I will."

I started the engine and signaled Pete to pull the wheel chocks. I quickly called the tower for taxi instructions and clearance to the duty runway. The tower cleared me for take-off and informed me that there were four airplanes at 15,000 feet about twenty miles to the Southwest. I continued my climb and took up a heading to the Southwest. As I was climbing, I armed my guns and gave them a short test. All seemed to be operating correctly.

I passed through fifteen thousand feet and continued up to seventeen thousand feet. I wanted an advantage if I could get it and if they were hostile. I wondered if I was being tracked by radar.

"Commander, the aircraft are turning to the North and climbing."

That left me with little doubt about their having radar. They did have it. I applied more power and climbed as fast as I could. I wanted to stay above them.

The radio came to life, and I heard. "Good morning, Commander, how are you this fine morning?"

I knew it had to be the German Major I had met yesterday. "Good morning, Major. It is nice to see you up early and enjoying the day."

"Thank you, Commander. I trust you are doing the same?"

"I was until something interrupted my breakfast."

"Please accept my apology, Commander. Would you like to continue breakfast at my place?"

"Thank you, Major, but something has come up."

"I must insist, Commander."

"And if I don't, Major?"

We were both like prizefighters, dancing around the ring, sizing each other up. They were in one part of the sky, and I was in the other.

"Commander, I would like to be very serious if you will allow me to."

"Major, you impress me as being an honorable man. Tell me what you are thinking."

"Commander, it is something I would like to talk to you about in person."

"That may be hard to do, Major."

"I will offer you safe conduct to my base, and you will not be detained when you are ready to leave. I hope we can work something out."

"I have a better proposition, Major."

"Tell me what it is, please."

"If you will send your friends home, I will meet you at the place we had our meeting yesterday. We can talk there."

"Commander, I have a friend I want you to meet."

"Major, you can bring your friend along. I also have a friend I would like to bring along. It would be just the four of us."

I don't think I can convince my friend. He does not want to leave our home. He has people he must avoid."

"Major, can you hold for a while. I need to talk to our base.

I switched my radio to our base frequency. "Rutling, I need to talk to President Villa. Can you get him on the radio?" I knew President Villa had a radio in his office he could talk on.

"Give me a minute, please," he replied.

"In a short time, I heard. "This is President Villa."

"Sir, this is Commander Baker, the airplanes on the radar are the people we talked to yesterday. The Major has asked me to accompany him back to his base. He indicated he would like to talk to me. He has guaranteed me safe passage, and I do believe him. Do I have your permission to do so?"

"Commander, I don't feel that it is a good idea. I am not sure they can be trusted. I cannot give you permission."

"Yes, Sir. I will inform him that I do not have permission."

I switched back to the frequency the Major was on. "Major, I did not receive permission. I am afraid I won't be able to accommodate you."

"I am sorry to hear that, Commander. I would have liked to talk to you. I do have something you may agree to."

"What is that, Major?"

"I will meet you at another airfield if you will do that. It is in the interest of avoiding any future conflict. I don't want to talk on the air where everyone can hear us."

"Where would you suggest, Major?"

"We could meet here and agree on a place. That should make it safe for both of us."

"I think I can do that, Major."

"Can you be here at 1100 hours tomorrow, Commander?"

"I will be here. If I can't get permission to do so, I will tell you at that time. We will have to work something else out if that is the case. I will see you tomorrow, Major."

"I look forward to it, Commander."

As I returned to Rutling, I tried to think about what he might want. I was trying to convince myself that they wanted to end hostilities and create a better relationship. I would talk to President Villa. I will need his permission anyway.

After I landed at Rutling, I went directly to see President Villa. I found him waiting for me. He had been informed about my conversation with the German Major.

As I entered his residence, Mia was there to greet me. "Bob, my Father, is waiting to talk to you, he knew you would be coming to see him."

"Thanks, Mia. Is our date still on for later? Everything must work around that, even if we must stop the world from turning."

"I don't think we need to go to that extreme, but, yes, it is still on, and I am looking forward to it.

"Mia, you are the main person in my life right now. Nothing else matters to me."

"Thank you, Bob, please don't stop the world from turning, I will comply peacefully."

President Villa was waiting for me at his office. "Come in, Bob." It was the first time he called me Bob. I was somewhat surprised. "I did not hear the conversation you had in the air, but it sounds as though it may have been an interesting one."

"It was indeed, Sir. I hope you can help me read between the lines."

"Bob, I am not entirely sure what it is. The Major's superior's reluctance to leave his base must be founded on the fact that he is a war criminal and does not want to get away from his safe spot, so to speak."

"I gave that a lot of thought too, Sir. I am not at all sure what the major wants to talk about."

"From what I hear, Bob, I think there is an excellent possibility they are trying to entice you away from us."

"I don't think I am that important, Sir. The only thing I can do is fly, and they have enough pilots. They don't need anymore."

"Believe me, Bob. Flying is not the only thing you can do, and they know it. You certainly can fly very well, which is a good enough reason in itself. I want to get some other people's input on this. You have my permission to meet this Major unless I inform you otherwise."

"I will do that, Sir. I would like to spend some time with Mia today if you have no objections."

"I have none whatsoever. I certainly approve of it, and I know her mother does too. I think she kind of likes you. Enjoy the rest of the day. We will talk tomorrow at eight."

"Thank you, Sir," I said as I left the room.

I found Mia in another office. I told her I asked her Father if it was all right if I spent some time with her.

"What did he say?"

"Mia, he told me to keep my hands off you, you were too good for me."

"Bob, you lie. My father thinks you are perfect and would never say that. Besides, my permission is the one you will need, not anyone else."

"I can toss in another one if I need to."

"And who's would that be."

"It is actually an important one."

"I suppose it is yours."

"That one is essential, but I was referring to your Mothers permission."

"You finally made some sense. Now go get cleaned up, so we don't waste the entire day."

"Mia, now that I have everyone's permission, I am filled with confidence."

"You must assume you have mine. Don't be too sure of yourself. You're not completely cleared yet."

I went back to my quarters to clean up. I thought I didn't know what Mia would want to do. I may need to put a suit on if she wants to go to someplace fancy. I thought I better give her a call and ask. "Mia, this is Bob. I didn't ask where you wanted to go. Do I need to put on a suit?"

"No, Bob, I want you to put on your uniform. I don't want to be seen with just anyone. I want to show you off."

"Do I need to, Mia. I am a little self-conscious in my uniform. I would rather wear a suit and be less conspicuous. Besides, all the girls will want to take me away from you. I don't want to deprive you of such great company. I will wear my uniform, but it will be your loss."

"I'll take the chance, Romeo. I can put some blinders on you so you will only be able to look at me."

"That won't be necessary, Mia, you are the only one I will see no matter who is there."

"That was sweet of you. I think I may be weakening just a tiny bit. I will see you in a short while."

I did dress in my uniform as requested and drove back over to pick Mia up. She was ready and waiting. I, again, marveled at her beauty. "Are you ready to go? By the way, where are we going?"

"I am going to show you some of Rutling's more interesting attractions. After which I have some friends, I would like you to meet. I have arranged for two of my friends to meet us at a little café in the old district of Rutling. It is a reminder of early life here. I would like to drive if you don't mind since I know my way around."

"I don't mind a bit; it will allow me to look around more at the attractions, especially the one with me."

"Am I being classified as an attraction."

I couldn't help but smile. "Not only an attraction, but you are also the main attraction."

"Thank you."

Mia offered me a fascinating tour of the older parts of Rutling. As expected, Rutling, in its early years, relied on the sea for its subsistence. The piers and seaside depicted life as it was many years ago. Still bustling with fishing boats and seaside restaurants. Some still as they were so long ago. We continued our tour. There was a dormant volcano that rose high to greet the heavens. Evidence of its activity so long ago was still present. No one was sure when it was last active. It must have been before man kept such records.

We followed the coastline for several miles, stopping at a seaside village that time seemed to have forgotten. Mia pulled up to a quaint building and parked. "This is where we will meet my friends. I am sure they will be here soon."

We departed our car and walked into a rustic ornate restaurant. Many antiques decorated the walls, reminding everyone of the life of yesteryear. Mia was immediately recognized, "Please come in, Miss Villa, your table is ready, come this way, please." We were ushered to a waiting table tucked away in a cozy corner.

The waiter must have been aware that we would be meeting someone. Would you care for some refreshments while you are waiting, Miss Villa?"

Mia turned and looked at me as if to tell me to order. "Please order first, Mia, what are you going to have?"

"I think I will have a glass of Chardonnay."

The waiter turned and looked at me. "That sounds like an excellent choice. I will have the same, please. The waiter departed only to return with a bottle of wine; he showed it to me for my approval. After I had given him my approval, he opened the bottle, poured us both a glass, and deposited the remainder in a bucket that had been placed beside our table.

"Bob, we can have a light lunch here if you wish. We can have dinner later."

"That sounds perfect, Mia."

We engaged in a light conversation until Mia noticed her friends had arrived. She gave them a wave that they returned. When they arrived at our table, I was introduced to Mike and Robin Kingsley. Robin and Mia had been best friends since their childhood. Robin had married Mike, who she met in the US while going to college. Mike was an engineer and had accepted a job with the Rutling government.

I immediately liked Robin and knew I would be good friends with Mike. We had a great lunch together. Mia asked them to accompany us this afternoon and join us for dinner later. They did accept and accompanied us on the rest of the tour, which was not very long considering the time we spent visiting in the quaint little restaurant.

The evening went well, but it did not seem to last long enough. Mia was an excellent dancer and accepted my lack of talent. When I was dancing close to her, I had a wonderful feeling come over me. I don't think I could even explain it. I could not help but tell her. "Mia, I have only known you a few days, and yet, I have a feeling that scares me. I know what it is, but I can't feel this way now. It's not fair to you. I don't want to hurt you, and I don't want to be hurt. I have a terrible feeling that is where we are going and the way it will end. My future is very cloudy and also very uncertain in many respects."

"Don't say that, Bob. Your future is what you will make it be. I don't know you well enough to tell you what to do. I hope you will stay around and see what happens. I know I like you and I think you like me. That seems like a good place to start."

"You are right, Mia. Maybe I will win a lottery or something big like that. Perhaps I already have and just don't realize it. I better buy a bunch of tickets."

"You will only need one, Bob."

"Thank you for reminding me, Mia."

We all decided to conclude the evening and made plans for another get-together. Mia drove me back to my car at her place and asked me to come in for a cup of coffee. I told her I had better get some sleep since I had to meet her father in the morning. I had not told her all that had taken place and what was planned for tomorrow.

"I understand, Bob. Maybe you will ask me out again sometime," she said in a joking manner.

"I think that is a very strong possibility. I hope you will accept."

"I think that is a very strong possibility also."

I felt Mia move close to me. I put my arms around her, pulled her closer, and whispered in her ear. "Do you mind if I like you a lot?"

"Let me give that some thought, Bob. "OK, No, I don't mind, do you mind if I like you a lot."

"I don't think I need to think about it, Mia. I can give you a very strong 'No.' I can tell you I don't mind without giving it any thought."

Mia put her arms around me as we shared a very passionate kiss. We bid each other good night as we parted.

As I drove back to my quarters, I couldn't help but think about Mia and where we were. I knew we had only known each other for a few days, but I don't think I have ever been more sure of anything in my life. Maybe I am now afraid of dying because I have a valid reason not to. I don't think the fear of dying was a presence in my life before, but I think it could be now. That is not good if you go into combat that way. If you are afraid, you make mistakes, and mistakes are all too often fatal.

I began to think I should tell President Villa that I want out, I don't want to fight his battles, but I did want his daughter. Maybe I should tell Mia that we should not see each other until this is over, but then I may lose her all the way. I guess I would have to bite the bullet and play out this hand. I didn't see any other way, but I had to chuckle just a bit. I could be a dead hero. Or I could be a live coward. I didn't intend to be a live coward, and I sure didn't like the other idea. I knew there was no in-between.

CHAPTER IX

I was up early and ate breakfast in a cafeteria that was in the building. I thought I would find President Villa to see if he had any thoughts he would like to share with me before I left.

I wanted an excuse to see Mia. I was not disappointed. I found Mia having coffee with her father and mother in a familiar sitting room. It was rather early, so I ask if I was interrupting anything. They said no and asked me to join them.

Mia asked me if I had any plans for today. I told her I was going to fly around for a while and kind of look things over. I did not think I needed to make her worry, so I did not tell her where I was going or what I would be doing. I asked President Villa if he would give me a few minutes of his time before I left. This whole set up is so bazaar. "Certainly, Bob, let's go down to my office."

After we arrived at his office, I asked. "Sir, I need your input on this situation. I want to know if I see the situation as it is."

"Bob, I will sum it up as how I perceive the situation to be. The group of Germans in Venezuela is allowed to stay there because of the large German population in that country. They do not want hostilities to originate from their country, so that is putting pressure on the group to relocate. They have chosen Rutling as the place they would like to relocate to. There are war criminals among them, and they are afraid that the US will come after them to prosecute them. They fear that Venezuela will allow this to happen. Not wanting to risk that possibility, they want to be in a place where they have more latitude. They feel that the US will not risk ravaging a country such as Rutling, so they would have a false sense of security if they can relocate to Rutling. They don't realize they are doomed because they will be made to pay for the crimes they have committed. Are you with me so far?"

"I am, Sir. Please continue."

"I don't feel we are in danger of being attacked here in Rutling. That would preclude all they are trying to do. They must find another way. When you intervened on your way down here, I am sure they wanted to take my family hostage and me. They thought they could then negotiate an agreement to let them come to Rutling. You stopped that. You now stand in their way. They feel they must compromise you to continue." President Villa hesitated and looked at me as if to question how I was accepting all this.

"Sir, do you think they will try to eliminate me?

"That is a necessity. I think they will try to get you to come over to their side. If you don't, they will have to get rid of you in some way. They have one big problem."

"What is that, Sir?"

"You are a US Navy officer. They know what will happen if they harm you. They simply can't afford to do that. They must find another way to eliminate you. The best way is to get you to come over to their side. If they fail to do this, they are at a standstill. I am not sure what will then follow. I would hope they would forget about Rutling, but desperate people do desperate things."

"What are your thoughts on my meeting today with the Major?"

"Bob, I think he will try to get you to be sympathetic to their cause. If that fails, he may offer you a bribe, a very substantial bribe. If that fails, and I am sure it will, I am not sure what will happen. I don't want you to be harmed. I have gotten to like you too much, and Mia would never forgive me, nor would I forgive myself. I have mixed feelings about you seeing him today. I will leave that up to you."

"Sir, I think I will be safe, and I would like to hear what he has to say. You know I would never forsake you for any reason."

"That is something I am very sure of, Bob."

"Sir, I have become very fond of Mia. I will never do anything to hurt her, and I will protect her with my life."

"I do not doubt that, Bob. I am sure Mia has become fond of you also. Her mother and I are fond of you, as well."

"I don't think I need to reaffirm how I feel about both of You, Sir."

"Thank you. Bob, take care of yourself. If you change your mind about going, it is perfectly all right with me. I was going to stop you from going, but you may accomplish something.

I left the room and walked down to the sitting room Mia and her mother were. I just told them I was leaving and wanted to say goodbye.

"Is everything alright, Bob?"

"Everything is fine."

"You're not going to do anything dangerous, are you, Bob?"

"I am going to be flying if you consider that dangerous."

Mia stood up and walked over to me. She put her arms around my neck and said. "Are you sure?"

"Yes, I am sure."

Mia had a very somber face. "I will miss you. Come back to me, Bob."

"I will, Mia."

I said goodbye and left.

When I arrived at the airfield, Pete was standing next to my plane and greeted me. "Good morning, Commander. I have your plane ready and armed, Sir."

"Thank you, Pete. How are things going for you today?"

"Just fine, Sir."

Pete helped me get into my plane, then stood by with a fire extinguisher as I started the engine. I signaled for Pete to pull the wheel chocks so I could begin my taxing. He waved as I started for the runway. I waved back. I had gotten taxi instructions and clearance for takeoff before. After I went through my pre-takeoff check, I moved onto the runway and started my takeoff. The plane gracefully lifted off the ground and started its upward climb. I glanced at my watch and saw that I had about 30 minutes until I was to meet the Major.

I began to mentally go over what I thought I could expect and what I would say or do. As I was doing this, a call came for me. "Commander Baker, this is Major Shultz, over."

"Good morning, Major, this is Commander Baker, over."

"How are you this morning, Commander?

"I'm doing good, Major, how are you?"

"Fine, Commander. Do you have a preference where you would like to meet?"

"You are more familiar with the region, Major, do you have a preference?"

"We could meet at Aruba, which is close. Will that work?"

"That will work for me, Major."

By this time, I had located him and was moving in on his right wing. He waved as he looked at me, so I returned the wave. We continued until we reached our destination. The Major called the tower for landing permission and instructions, and we continued into the break and landed. I wondered what the people on the ground thought as they watched a German ME-109 and a US P-51 come into the break together.

After landing, the Major was directed and stopped a short distance from a nearby hanger. I pulled up and stopped a short distance away. We departed our planes and met in the middle. After greeting each other, I asked him where he would like to go to talk.

"Commander, let's go see if there is a coffee shop in the main building."

"Good, Major, I could use a cup of coffee." We walked over to the building, suggested by the Major, and went in. We found a coffee shop, so we seated ourselves.

"Major, what do you have on your mind?"

"First of all, I want you to know who we are."

"I think I already know that, Major."

"If you think there are men among us who are evading the US, you are right, but I am not one of them. I was invited to come along. I had very little left in Germany, so I decided to go. They would pay me and offer a safe place for me to stay. I had nothing to lose."

"Major, didn't you think you would be assumed to be as guilty as they were, and be prosecuted along with them?"

"To tell the truth, Commander, I did not think that way. I felt I would be able to, at some time, be allowed to live a normal life. I think I have been wrong in that thinking."

"I think you are right in that assumption. How do I fit into this, or am I just the message boy?"

"I was told to offer you a large sum of money if you will step out of the picture. It is fifty thousand dollars."

"Major, I think you know I will not accept your offer. I am still in the US Navy, I am sympathetic with Rutling, and the money is stolen and tainted with blood."

"I knew that before I asked, Commander. They also wanted to invite you to join us. I told them this would be a mute question.

"You are right, Major, for the same reasons. You should join us instead."

"I wouldn't live very long if I did that. I do have one more offer."

"What is that, Major?"

"If the President of Rutling, will allow us to move to Rutling, we have access to untold wealth. We will share that with him."

"I will tell him, but I can tell you what he will say."

"You don't have to, Commander, I know the answer. The Major looked down at the ground. When he looked up, he continued. "I don't want to see you in combat, Commander. If you mark your plane, I will not shoot at you if it comes down to that."

"I don't want to shoot at you either, Major. I think you are an honorable man, but I will defend Rutling in any way I must. I would like to call you my friend, but I will put that in your hands. I wish you would think about what happened here today and make a better decision. Then we will be friends."

"I wish I could, Commander, but I think I will die in any case."

"I would prefer to die with honor, Major."

The Major just nodded, and we started for our planes.

As soon as I stepped out of the door, I saw another ME-109 sitting next to ours. What's going on, Major, is this a trick?

"No! I don't know what is going on. He must have followed me. Believe me, Commander, I had nothing to do with this. Stay back, please. I will see what is going on."

Major Shultz walked over to the other pilot who was standing by his plane. A lot of German talk erupted. It appeared the Major was furious. The other pilot saluted, turned, and started back to his plane.

The Major motioned me to come over. "Commander, he said he followed me to make sure I didn't get in any trouble. I am sorry, I had nothing to do with this. I hope you believe me."

"Right now, I don't know what to think. I trust you. I hope I am not wrong."

"You are not wrong, Commander. I hope the next time we meet it will be as friends. Good luck to you."

"I hope that also. Time will tell." I shook hands with the Major and started for my plane.

The Major took off ahead of me. I waited for the prop wash from his plane to dissipate. I then taxied onto the runway. Everything appeared to be OK, so I advanced the throttle and started my takeoff roll. I was airborne about halfway down the runway. As I gained altitude, I moved the landing gear handle to the up position and heard the gear doors close after the wheels were seated in the wells. I suddenly heard a loud explosion followed by fire erupting from my engine. I felt metal hit my left arm and leg. I didn't feel any pain; I just felt the concussion. I didn't have time to do anything except try to get back control of my plane. I had a limited amount of power and control, so I came down hard on the runway. The fire had only lasted an instant and gone out. My control panel was in shambles. I was trying to stay conscious as I slid off the runway throwing grass and dirt over my windscreen. I couldn't see, my goggles were covered with dirt and grass, my oxygen mask had taken the blow and was then ripped from my face. It had absorbed the shock. I was thankful for that.

The plane had come to a stop, and I was still conscious. I knew fire could erupt at any moment, so I unbuckled myself and tried to stand up. I couldn't get up, so I released the chute harness to free myself and was able to stand up enough to slide over the side. That was the last I remember.

Later they told me I was out for several hours. When I woke up, I saw a blur around me that appeared to be people. When I was able to focus, I discovered ladies dressed in white, looking at me. I heard one of them say something in Spanish to someone in the room. A doctor came over to me and spoke to me in English. "How are you doing? Can you tell me your name?"

"I looked bewildered for a short time and answered, "Bob."

"Well, Bob, you had a nasty accident. You are very fortunate to have had on goggles and an oxygen mask. Your face and head came out OK, but you did get some damage to your left arm and leg. Nothing we can't fix, but you won't be flying for a while." The Doc could see I was still a bit confused, so he just told me to get some rest, and he would see me later. I think I drifted off and lost contact with the real world.

Back at Rutling, Mia had been shopping. When she returned, she walked to her fathers' office and asked him if Bob was back.

"I haven't seen him yet, Mia. He was going to meet someone on another island, so maybe he got to talking too long. I will call the airfield and see if they have been in contact with him."

President Villa, called the airfield while Mia was still in his office. "This is President Villa, have you been in contact with Commander Baker?"

"Mr. President, we have not had any contact with Commander Baker since he left about three hours ago."

"Try to contact him on the radio and get back to me."

"Yes, Sir," he replied.

Thirty minutes went by before the airfield called President Villa back. "Mr. President, this is Rutling airfield. We have tried to contact Commander Baker, but he does not answer. We checked with Air Traffic Control, and they do not have any missing planes. Sorry, Sir."

About that time, Mia walked into the office. "What did you find out, Dad."

"Mia, we can't find out where he is. I am sure he must have just talked too long and forgotten about the time."

"That is not like Bob, Dad. You know he would never do that. Mia started to cry, "I think something has happened to him."

"Mia, try to keep calm. I will check to see if anyone is reporting a downed plane. We have radio stations around the islands that would have gotten a distress call if one was put out. If they don't find one, I will have them call around to see if any of them heard a distress call."

"Mia had set down on a couch and was still crying. "I know he has crashed somewhere and is trouble. Please send out some boats to look for him"

"Mia, we wouldn't know where to look, it is a vast ocean. I think he just stayed too long and will call us soon."

Mia was desperate by this time. "Call someone, do something. Please."

President Villa spoke. "Mia, I will put every resource I have to work. Please calm down and give me a chance to get everyone alerted and working on it."

Mia was getting close to being hysterical by this time. The president had called his wife, Carman, and told her to get right down to his office. When she arrived, she, too, was crying and starting to get excited.

"Carman, try to calm Mia down. Bob is missing, and I am trying to find out where he is."

A call came into President's villa's office. "Mr. President, this is the airfield. We have been informed of an airplane accident on Aruba Island. We have not been able to confirm anything, but they think it was a P-51 that crashed on takeoff. We have not been able to contact Aruba, but we will keep trying."

"Let me know as soon as you get more news."

Meanwhile, Bob had again regained conciseness. This time he felt much more coherent. When he looked around, he saw Major Schultz standing by his bed. "Major, what happened?"

"You crashed on takeoff, Commander."

"I had an explosion in the engine. I don't think it was a natural explosion."

"I don't either, Commander. I think someone placed an explosive device under the engine cowling of your plane. I hate to say or think it, but it had to be the pilot from our group. I don't see how it could be anyone else."

"I need to ask you, Major. We're you aware that this would happen, or did you have anything to do with it?"

"I did not on both counts. I would never be a part of anything like this."

"I would like to believe you, Major. The fact that you are here is in your favor. I wonder if Rutling knows about what happened?"

"I will need to go back to my base. I will call Rutling and inform them of what took place after I am in the air. Who should I talk to?"

"Speak directly to President Villa. They can get him on your radio."

"I will do that, Commander. By the way, do you have a first name? Mine is Otto."

"Mine is, Bob."

"I will see you around, Bob." With that, Otto gave me a casual salute, which I returned.

Before he could leave, I added, "I'll see you around too, Otto." Somehow, I seemed to know I would see Otto again.

Otto did put a call out to Rutling after he was in the air.

"Rutling tower, this is Major Schultz, I have a message for President Villa. Can you relay it?"

"Roger, Major Schultz, I can connect you directly to President Villa if you wish."

"Rutling tower, please do that."

In a short time, he heard. "This is President Villa."

"President Villa, I am Major Schultz, the person Commander Baker met today. I have some news for you about Commander Baker."

"Please go on, is he OK?"

"Commander Baker is alright, he had an accident on Aruba today and did receive some injuries. They are not life-threatening. He asked me to inform you."

"Thank you, Major, thank you."

"You are very welcome. I do want you to know that I had no responsibility for what happened."

"What did happen, Major."

"It's a long story, Sir. I will let Commander Baker tell it to you." Major Schultz fell silent.

Mia and her mother had listened to the call from Major Schultz. Mia started crying, even more, fell into a chair, and murmured, "Thank you, God." Her mother sat down beside her and echoed what Mia had just said.

"Dad, can we go right now and get Bob? I want to see him as soon as I can. Please don't make me wait.

"Mia, I will need to find out what condition Bob is in and if he can be moved. It will be dark soon. I would rather wait till tomorrow and operate in the light."

"I really want to see Bob, Dad."

"Let me find out more, Mia. We will try to talk to him or maybe the Doctor that took care of him."

"OK, I will do as you say. Can you try him now?"

"President Villa called his secretary and told her to try to make contact with the hospital in Aruba. She should talk to the Doctor that took care of Bob, and lastly, we would speak to Bob if he was able to talk.

The secretary called back on the intercom in about fifteen minutes and told the President she had Dr. Clark on the phone. President Villa lost no time in retrieving his phone. "Hello, Doctor, this is President Villa from Rutling. I understand you have one of my pilots in your hospital."

I do, and he appears to be doing very well at this time. Would you like to talk to him, Sir?

"I would, Doctor, thank you."

"Hello, Mr. President, I am sorry to tell you I lost one of your airplanes today."

"What took place, Bob?"

I had a good, but nonproductive talk with Major, Schultz today."

"What happened?"

"I will tell you all about it when I get back. I don't think I should say too much over the phone,"

We will do that, Bob."

Mia was almost beside herself to talk to Bob, so the president knew he had to relinquish the phone or have it torn from his grip. "Here, Mia," and handed the phone to Mia.

"Bob, are you alright, how bad are you hurt?"

"I got cut up a little. I will be fine in a couple of weeks."

"Did you crash?"

"I did, Mia, but I came out of it all right. I will be back flying sooner than you think."

"I will ask Dad to have someone come get you the first thing tomorrow, so be ready."

"I should be all right to come home, I am sure. I will ask the Doc in the morning if it will be all right to release me. I am not hurt that bad, and I do want to see you."

"Bob, I thought I had lost you. I didn't think I could stand it if I did lose you. I may never let you out of my sight again. I may keep you with me forever."

"Mia, it was so sweet of you to say that. I may just hold you to what you said."

"I mean it, Bob. I will see you tomorrow."

"Goodbye, Mia. I can't wait until tomorrow."

CHAPTER X

I thought the morning would never come. I was that anxious to get back to see Mia. The doctor came in early and talked with me.

"Bob, they tell me someone will be here soon to pick you up. Your wounds are not as bad as I first thought. Some of the cuts were fairly deep, but they should heal quickly if you take care of them properly. I will send a note along with you for the doctor on Retling."

I interrupted, "How long do you think it will be before I can fly again?"

"Are you asking for this in a worst-case scenario?"

"I guess you could put it that way."

"Bob, my best guess would be in two to three weeks. That depends on a lot of assumptions. Try to delay it as long as possible. A lot of stress on your arm and leg could reopen the wounds. We don't want that to happen, do we?"

"Absolutely not, Doctor."

"It has been a pleasure meeting you, Bob. You are an amazing man. I wish you the best of luck."

"Thank you, Doctor. I also want to thank you for what you did for me."

"I do have one question if you don't mind my asking."

"Not at all, what is it?"

"I have a burning curiosity about the German officer flying the ME-109. You don't need to say anything if you would care not to."

"It's a very long story, Doctor. Briefly, when I first came here, we were adversaries. I shot him down when we confronted each other at our first meeting. Since then, in a strange twist of fate, we met on the ground and put our animosity behind us. We have become friends. I don't know if you know it, but it was a planted explosive device that brought me down. I, at first, though he was part of the plan to eliminate me, I feel certain now that he was not. If I had been much higher when the device went off, I wouldn't be here now. Maybe sometime, when this is all over, we can sit down with a cup of coffee, and I can tell you about it."

"I might hold you to that, Bob, right now, I better get some paperwork done and have someone get you ready to travel. Your ride could be here at any time." The Doctor stood up and left.

It wasn't long until a nurse came in to get me ready to travel. She had my flight suit with her. "We washed this for you, Mr. Baker. It does have some holes in it. If you would prefer to wear hospital surgical pants, I can get some for you."

The flight suit will be fine. Thank you."

"Can you stand up? I will help you put the suit on, so you don't fall."

"I won't know until I try." I was a little shaky, but I did manage to stand up, and with the nurse's help, I was able to dress. The nurse helped me to a chair where I sat down to wait.

"Will you be alright here, Mr. Baker?"

"I will be fine. Thank you for your help."

I tried to get comfortable while I sat there. My left arm was in a sling, so I couldn't move it too much. My leg was wrapped for support, and I had been given a cane to help me walk.

I didn't have to wait long. I heard a quiet tap on the door, followed by it opening slightly. I said, "Come in, please."

"Are you decent, Bob?"

"Come in, Mia. I didn't expect you to be here. You should have stayed at home. I don't like to see you flying with things the way they are."

"Dad didn't want me to go either, but I insisted. Don't get up, Bob."

I complied as Mia crossed the room and threw her arms around me. She was crying and seemed not to want to let me go. Mia just held on to me and kept sobbing.

"Mia, don't cry. I'm all right. I just got a few scratches. If you don't stop, you may get me crying too. I can't let that happen."

"I can't help it. I just want to hang on to you forever and never let you out of my sight again."

Someone came into the room, hesitated when they saw Mia crying, and stood silent for a short time.

Finally, Mia stood up. "I think I will be alright now." The person that had entered was the nurse that was here earlier. She had a wheelchair for me to use to get to the plane.

"Let me help you into the wheelchair, Mr. Baker, so we can take you out to your plane." I was able to stand with Mia's help and get into the chair. Mia wouldn't let go of me while the nurse was helping. The Nurse smiled and just kept doing what she had to do.

Getting into the plane was not the easiest. I had to climb several steps to get in, but we finally made it. I was seated and buckled myself in. Mia sat right across from me and buckled herself in also. The pilot asked if we were ready. After an affirmative answer, he started the plane and taxied out to the duty runway.

It didn't take long to get to Rutling. When we pulled up to the main building at Rutling, I saw that President Villa and his wife Carman were there. I received a very warm welcome from both of them. We then drove back to their residence, which was only a short distance away. I was sure I would be in for an untold number of questions, so I just braced myself and waited.

Instead, President Villa just said to me. "Bob, I know you must be tired. We will wait and talk tomorrow. You can spend some time with Mia and rest for now."

"Thank you, Sir. I am rather tired."

As the President was leaving, he told Mia to have me stay in one of the guest rooms tonight, so I would have help if I needed it.

Mia asked. "Bob, have you had anything to eat today?"

"I did have some coffee earlier this morning, but nothing since."

"I haven't eaten either. We can have something now if you wish."

"That does sound good to me, Mia. I think I need to kick back for a while. I feel a little on the weak side."

"I'll help you down to the lounge and have something prepared for us. You can use one of the recliners, so it will be more comfortable for you while we are waiting for our food."

Mia made sure I was comfortable, then left to have something prepared for us. When she returned, I was asleep in my recliner. She woke me so I could eat, and offered to find me something to wear instead of my torn flight suit. She was able to procure some sleepwear and a housecoat. With help from an aid, I did get them on.

After eating, I pushed back in my recliner. Mia put a cover on me and allowed me to drift off once again. The last thing I remember was Mia holding my hand. It was undoubtedly the company and security I needed.

Mia spent the entire next day with me in the lounge. I know I was very weak and drifted off in short naps. I don't think she hardly left my side. At one point, a doctor checked me over and prescribed what he thought I should have.

Early in the evening, Mia helped me to my room, helped me get into bed, and stayed with me, just talking, until I again drew very weary.

Before she left, she told me she would stay with me if I wanted her to. "That's not necessary, Mia. I'll be all right. I may need to use the restroom, but I think I can manage."

Mia left the room and returned with a little bell for me to ring if I needed something. She informed me she would have a recliner moved into my room and stay so she would hear the bell when I rang it.

"Don't do that, Mia. You need your rest too. I don't want you to run yourself down and get sick."

"I just want to be close to you, Bob."

"I will allow you to move a recliner in and stay with me for a while. I like having you near me too, Mia."

Mia had someone move the recliner into my room and place it next to my bed. She sat down, reached over, and took my hand. Her hand was soft and warm. She held my hand firmly and drew it to her cheek and gently caressed my hand with her cheek. An odd feeling came over me. I wanted to tell her I was falling in love with her, but I knew it was too soon. I wanted to be sure. A few days did not seem to be enough time.

"Bob."

"What is it, Mia?"

"Will you laugh at me if I tell you something?"

"Of course not."

"When I was a little girl, I use to look at the sky and watch the little white clouds sailing by. Some looked like angels, some I tried to imagine as a knight on a white horse that was coming to rescue me and carry me off to a land filled with dreams. A land filled with dreams that all came true. I was wondering if you could be that knight. You came from the sky and rescued me from a fiery dragon that was spitting fire at me. You know what I mean, the German airplanes."

"No matter how much I would like to be that knight, Mia, I am not sure I am worthy of such an honor. If it makes sense to you, I will graciously accept that honor and make you indebted to me for the rest of your life. But, if I carry you off, I have no intention of bringing you back or releasing you ever again."

"That is the way my dream goes, so I would have to accept that fate, Bob."

"Each day, I ask myself, who is Mia, where did she come from? Now I know. You are the other white cloud, the one you thought was an Angel. You simply must be an Angel; I know you are not a real person. You are either an Angel or a dream. I live in fear of waking up and finding that you were a dream, and you don't exist. I am afraid I will wake up, and you will be gone. I don't want that to happen, Mia. I don't want to lose you."

"Bob, I think we have something good going. Why can't we just accept it and see where it will go. We hardly know each other, let's just be friends for now and see what happens."

"I am sure you are right, Mia. I live in fear that I will have to leave, and I will never see you again."

"We do have some control over our future and have the ability to change it. For now, Bob, just let us like each other and see where it will go."

"That sounds like a wonderful idea, Mia. Alright, I like you and want to spend more time with you. Mind if I like you a lot, or am I limited to just liking you."

"We can like each other a lot, that will be alright with me."

"When can I start to like you just a little more, Mia?"

"I think you will know when that happens, but if you don't, I will let you know."

"I'll be looking forward to that time, Mia."

We talked for a rather long time until Mia thought she better leave and let me get some rest. She gave me a gentle kiss and walked out of the room.

After I had rested, the rest of the day was spent in a relaxed atmosphere. The night went well with me waking up feeling much stronger. I was ready to talk to President Villa whenever he was ready.

About mid-morning, President Villa sent word that he would like to talk to me whenever I felt I was up to it. He had procured a wheelchair for me, so I would not have to put any unneeded stress on my injured leg. I did go to his office as soon as I received that information.

I knocked on his door and heard him say, "Come in, Bob."

After exchanging our pleasantries, we had a full discussion of the events of yesterday. I told the President that I was sure it was an explosive device of some kind that brought me down. I felt quite certain it was the other German pilot that planted it. I was sufficiently sure that Major Schultz was not a part of it. I would continue to trust him until I had further reason not to. President Villa would not take any further action at this time. He would, however, notify the US Navy what had happened. I told the President that I would be required to make a report as well and would do so.

President Villa then informed me that four of the new pilots had reported in, and the rest should be here in the next two days. "When you feel up to it, Bob, I would like you to take charge of them and do whatever you need to do to get them organized."

"Sir, I will send word for them to be at our headquarters at 0100 and meet with them. I need to make sure all are in the right position and get them started with their indoctrination."

"Let me know how it goes and what you think of them when you can. The incident you just had will undoubtedly be cause for more tension between our two groups. I would like your input and will talk to you later to see if and what you think we should do. Give it some thought."

"I will, Sir. I will also give you an assessment of the new pilots and what I plan to do."

"Thank you, Bob, you can contact me whenever you want."

I then left the President's office and started the ball rolling.

The pilots that had reported in were two Canadian pilots, one British, and one American. The other two that were still to report in were both American pilots.

I did meet with them at 0100. I decided not to go into depth until the other two had arrived. I had some reservations on how they would get along and brought that point up. I would take a much harder stance on that when we all met later.

From what I was told, the other two pilots would be here this afternoon or tomorrow morning. I scheduled a meeting for 0200 for the day after tomorrow.

I also received a dispatch from Admiral Dean, telling me to stand down and not initiate any action of any kind. If it could be proven that the organization in Venezuela did make an attempt on my life, we had what we needed to go after them. Because I was a United States military officer, it would be considered a direct attack on our armed forces. It would have to start with our confronting Venezuela for harboring these criminals. Admiral Dean emphasized that we wanted to bring these war criminals to justice.

I did decide to meet individually with the pilots that were here, and I told them all to be at our headquarters at 0800 tomorrow morning.

I spent the rest of the day with Mia and her mother. Dinner that evening included President Villa and was void of current events.

I did go to our headquarters the following morning. I left the wheelchair behind and opted to use my cane, not wanting to appear as an invalid. I tried to appear rugged and up to the task at hand.

I first met with each pilot individually. I wanted to size each one up and make sure they had an acceptable reason for being here. I found that the Canadian had lost a friend due to a German pilot. He had nothing but revenge on his mind and wanted to kill as many Germans as he could. I did not wish to have a loose cannon in our ranks. He would only spell trouble. When I told him I could not use him, he became irate and even threatened me. I told him he would be compensated for his inconvenience and asked him to leave, which he finally did.

The two men from Britain were just a couple of street thugs. I felt they would be nothing but troublemakers. I had the sense that they would not follow orders and cause problems where ever they could. I knew they did not have the proper discipline and would be almost impossible to control. Neither had the necessary experience I also needed. They also were dismissed.

The remaining three American pilots all had a lot of experience. One was an Ace, while the other two both had scored victories in the air. They appeared to be well disciplined. Two had flown the P-51 while the other had experience in the P-47 Thunderbolt and P-38 Lightning. I could not have been more pleased and felt very good about them.

Jim and Pat were the two P-51 pilots, and Mike was the last.

Jim had held the rank of Major and was the Ace. I knew he was well qualified, so I placed him in charge of the other two and responsible for getting Mike qualified in the P-51. I would meet with them each day and oversee their progress. I wanted them to fly together as much as possible to get to know how everyone thought and reacted to all situations. I intended to join them as soon as possible.

I constantly kept in touch with President Villa. He was also in contact with Admiral Dean and working with him in every way he could. I did tell him of my decision with the pilots, which he was in full agreement with. I told him that, with the US involved at a higher level, it was not necessary to have as many pilots as had been previously thought. I told him that four of us could deflect anything spontaneous from the opposition. President Villa agreed.

When I left President Villa's office, I ran into Mia. She immediately confronted me. "Bob, where is your wheelchair?"

"I felt I could get along all right with my cane. I didn't want to look like an invalid to my new pilots."

"You should be using your wheelchair. You want to have some complications and be stuck in bed?"

"Of course, I don't. I don't want to look weak to my pilots either."

Mia just looked at me with a very disgusting look and tilted her head as if to show her disapproval further.

"I will try to do better, Mia."

"I will accept that for now. Robin called and wanted to know if we would meet them later for dinner."

"Must I go in my wheelchair, or am I permitted to use a cane?"

"Since I will be there to help you, you can use your cane if you let me help you."

"I don't think I have been given a choice, so I will accept your kind offer."

"I will call Robin and see where she would like us to meet. Do you have a preference for what you would like to have for dinner?"

"Your choice, Mia. I do like seafood, but you must have a lot of that, so I will let you choose."

"I always like seafood, but I will let Robin and Mike select where we will eat. I will call her and tell her to choose, but to make it a place where you can get around with your cane."

"That's not necessary, but as you wish."

Mia left the room and came back a short time later. "Robin has suggested we come over to their home. She said it would be a lot more comfortable. She also wanted to know what happened to you. I just told her you had been in an accident. Be prepared to answer a lot of questions."

"Maybe Robin will have more sympathy for me than you are showing."

I received a very disgusting look from Mia. I knew I had to backtrack and fast. "I didn't mean that, Mia. It was just a bad joke. I could never have gotten more help and sympathy from anyone else. Then I got it from you. That was a joke, but I could never tell you how much it meant to me."

"That is much better, Bob."

"Thank you, Mia. You best be careful, I may fall in love with you before I am allowed to."

We did go to Robin and Mike's. We had not only a wonderful dinner but an enjoyable evening as well. I could easily see why Mia and Robin were such close friends. I think Mike and I will be good friends as well. That is if I am allowed to stay in this part of the world. I know it will take a lot of good fortune for this to happen. I feel more and more attracted to Mia and hope she is doing the same.

There is so much that must go right to make that happen. Mia is a religious girl and has the same devotion to the Holy Mother that I do. It bonds us together, both in faith and family values. Family values that are promoted by faith. She is a copy of her parents, who instilled those values in her. Her father, President Villa, governs this island with love for his people. His leadership is reflected in love from those he governs. He is, undoubtedly, one of the greatest men I have ever met."

I do have a problem I must deal with. I am now more solidly implanted in the US Navy. I know, if I stay in the Navy, I will have to leave here sometime soon. It is something I do not want to think about or deal with right now. I will just have to wait and see.

CHAPTER XI

The next few weeks seemed to pass without much happening. Admiral Dean had launched an investigation into what happened in Aruba. It was difficult to connect the organization in question to it, now code-named 'Zebra,' to that incident. We were confident that Zebra had been the guilty one, but it would be very difficult to prove.

Zebra had been very quiet since that time. I am sure they did not want attention directed to them. They would prefer that it just go away.

I told Admiral Dean I felt Zebra would drop their interest in Rutling to avoid any further friction between Rutling and them. They just could not afford to have any attention toward themselves.

I was back flying on a limited basis and had been working with my pilots. We had a great group. It was set up with me as the leader. Pat was my wingman, Jim was the section leader with Mike as his wingman. We were getting quite good at working together. I hoped we would not have to engage in combat, but if we did, we would be a formidable foe.

Mia and I continued to grow closer. We spent a lot of time with Robin and Mike. I knew I would have to talk to

Mia at some point about my future here on Rutling Island. I fought it within myself and tried to tell myself that it would solve itself, but deep down, I knew it wouldn't.

I had a call come in from Admiral Dean; it was on an encrypted line, so we felt we could talk openly.

After we made the connection, Admiral Dean went straight to the point. "Bob, we are getting nowhere trying to connect Zebra to the attempt on your life. We don't feel they will now initiate any hostility toward Rutling in fear of causing us to intervene. We feel Rutling is safe at this time, but we still want those war criminals. Do you have any ideas?"

"Admiral, I have three volunteer pilots with me now. They are good. We have perfected a team between us. We could try to entice them out, but I don't think we should enter Venezuela's air space. We could get everyone in a lot of trouble that way. I will do whatever you tell me to do."

"You're right. I don't think we can do that. We do want those war criminals. Perhaps, we will have to play a waiting game and hope they make a mistake. We could protest to Venezuela, but we don't have enough evidence to make a valid protest."

"Admiral, I have one outside thought. I believe Major Schultz and I have a good relationship. If I could talk to him, I may convince him to come over to our side. However, it is not very likely to happen. I am sure Zebra would try to eliminate him in retaliation. It is just a thought."

"Bob, I am sure you are right. We don't want to have Major Schultz eliminated, and I am sure that would very likely happen."

"I could try to catch one of their planes in international waters and engage him. I am sure he would try to avoid us, but it is a very outside chance."

"Bob, for now, try to keep patrols in the air as much as possible and hope they make a mistake. We do have operatives in their area. They may find a way to get to the war criminals. Play it low key for now."

"Yes, Sir. I will do that. I will contact you if anything changes."

"I will keep in contact with you too, Bob. Please bring President Villa up to date."

"Yes, Sir."

After we hung up. I sat there for a long time, wondering about this whole situation. One good thing did come from it. I will have a longer time to spend with Mia.

As soon as I could, I visited President Villa and filled him in on what the Admiral and I had talked about.

I also talked to my pilots. I instructed them to have a designated pilot and plane ready twenty-four hours a day. We would have a pager that would be passed to the designated pilot. He was to keep himself available and ready to fly within a reasonable time. If anything suspicious showed up, he was to check it out. I also wanted us to operate as much as possible, trying to stay out of Venezuela's air space, but close enough to entice someone from Zebra to come out. I put Jim in charge of seeing that this was complied with. It would be a cat and mouse game with very high stakes. I did ask and received President Villa's permission.

I told my pilots not to initiate any action. Try to get them to act first without putting themselves in harm's way. They were to fight back only if the other pilot made a hostile gesture first, and they could not avoid it. I didn't want to lie about anything. If you don't lie, you will keep it right each time it is repeated.

I started to leave but decided to get some flight time in, so I ventured back to our squadron area. I found my pilots in the ready room, getting ready to go out on a flight. I changed their plan, saying that we would go out in pairs and patrol the area and sweep the coast of Venezuela, staying in international waters. I notified radar to let us know what was in the air and what they thought it was. We did have a couple of calls from our radar station for something to check out, but nothing out of the ordinary turned up.

After landing, I had some paperwork to do and thought it was a good time to do it. I also wanted to talk to President Villa again to keep him up to date on what was going on. It would also allow me to see Mia.

My meeting with the President was rather short since I did not have a lot more to report. I did find Mia and took enough time with her for a cup of coffee. After this, I asked her if she would care to have dinner with me later.

"I would like to, Bob, but I do have a date this afternoon and not sure when I will be back."

I know I must have looked rather startled when she said date. I just said, "Oh," and stood there with a stupid look on my face.

"Is anything wrong, Bob?"

"No, I guess you just surprised me a little is all."

"This is an old friend I haven't seen for a while. He is only going to be here for a couple of days, and I would like to see him while he is here. Maybe we can have dinner Saturday night. Will that work for you?"

I was angry. I thought we had some sort of an understanding, but I guess it was a one-person understanding. I just happen to be that one person.

I told Mia, "I think I will be gone this weekend. I Don't plan to come back until Sunday."

"That is certainly too bad, where are you going?"

I was really between a rock and a hard place. I know, I stammered for a while. I finally got out. "I met someone while I was in Aruba. Someone I would like to see again."

"Who is that, Bob?"

"Just someone I met there."

Now it was Mia's turn to say, "Oh."

"Maybe we can get together the following weekend, Mia. I can pencil you in until you can check your datebook to see if you will be free."

"I will do that, Bob."

Mia's voice was just a little louder than usual. She just turned and walked away.

As I watched her walk away, I wondered what I had done. I was just plain jealous and did a stupid thing. I was hurt and couldn't believe she would date anyone else. Maybe it was all right for her to see an old friend. I guess it depends on what sort of an old friend he was. I thought she would have at least explained it to me. The worst part is that now I have to go to Aruba and stay overnight. I thought that maybe I could look up the doctor who helped me while I was there. He wanted to talk to me anyway, so this is just as good a time as any.

I had moved back to my old quarters, so I drove over there. I was still angry and wanted to let off some steam. My other pilots were there, so I asked them if they wanted to go out for a drink and grab dinner after. I received three eager responses. Jim, have one man on standby and in a condition to be able to fly. We decided to go as we were. There was a little bar I knew of that had a happy hour and close to the airfield, so we started there.

After an excellent start for the evening, I took them to the restaurant where Mia and I had met Robin and Mike. We walked in the door and were met by a hostess that escorted us to a table across the room. As we passed through the tables, I glanced over and saw Mia with her date at a nearby table. I hesitated long enough to wave at her, then kept going. She only raised her hand about half of the way up before I was gone.

I was seated with my back to the table at which Mia and her date were, so I did not see her get up and approach our table. I just heard someone say, Bob. I jerked my head around and saw Mia standing there.

I stood up as she took hold of my hand. All I heard was, "Dance with me."

"Bob, why are you being so rude to me?"

"Mia, you were on a date. I did not think it would be appropriate for me to stop and talk to you."

"He is just a friend, Bob."

"Mia, friends date friends. Didn't you tell me we were friends? We dated as friends. I thought you had another friend that you must like more as a friend than me. I apologize if I did not understand the ground rules."

"Bob, you are being ridiculous.

"I'm sorry, Mia. That is the way I saw it this afternoon and the way I see it now."

"Before I take you over and introduce you to my friend, I want you to promise me you will come over and see me before you leave tomorrow. Will you promise me you will do that?"

"If you want me to come over, I will."

"I truly want you to come over, Bob. Now let me take you over to meet James."

As we approached their table, Mia introduced me to her friend James.

"James and I grew up together about a block apart. His wife, Nancy, was one of my best friends. They are going to have their first wedding anniversary soon. James wants to get Nancy something special. He wants my advice on it, so I agreed to help him approve a piece of jewelry he has selected and has with him. If I don't like it, he knows Nancy will not either."

"Mia, I hope you will forgive me. James, I needed to apologize. I thought Mia had found a new boyfriend and was dropping me. I was rather upset."

"Bob, take my advice and don't let this lovely lady get away. She has told me all about you."

"There are a lot of bumps in the road, James. I am not sure it is best for Mia. I need to think of Mia before myself."

We said goodbye. I told Mia I would see her tomorrow and went back over to the table where my pilots were.

Suddenly, everything had changed. It was like walking out of the dark of night into the warmth of sunshine. I couldn't help but say a little prayer of thanks.

We had an excellent dinner, even the food taste better, and we had a very productive evening. I think I got to know my pilots better and learned more about each one on an individual base. Each one had a story all its own. Most had been driven here by a major, or series of significant happenings in their life. All appeared to be Christian men who came from a Christian background. None were bent on killing. As far as I could see, none had a death wish, which is often all too common among men who deal with death often in their lifetime. None were married. All seemed as normal as one could be in the work they had chosen. All had a love for flying, although that is not what drove them to the work they had volunteered for. I do think they did share a common trait. That was the love of adventure.

It is difficult to read men such as this. I believe all had a spark inside of them that drove them into doing what they were doing. One thing they did have in common was the lack of fear. In combat, fear is the deadliest factor in the equation. It can kill you if you cannot overcome it. I had to tell myself that I had some of the greatest pilots in the world with me.

The next day was Saturday, so I thought I would drive over to see Mia and make sure I had presented the best apology possible. That and I wanted to see her again for a reason we often fell back on when we were young. That was "Just because." It was kind of a catchall reason.

Carmen answered the door and told me Mia was in the study reading. I made my way to where she was and knocked on the door. Mia opened the door and greeted me with a smile that blossomed into something warm and friendly. I was secretly hoping it was a message that she had forgiven me. "Hi, Mia, I had to come over and make sure you have forgiven me for the childish way I acted yesterday."

Mia smiled even more and started to say something. I put up my hand and stopped her. "Before you say anything or tell me to leave, I want to beg for your mercy and ask you to forgive me. I did not have a very good reason to act the way I did. I like you very much and can't bear the thought of not seeing you again. Will you please forgive me?"

"I may have to put you on probation for a while. I will give it some serious thought. Please come in. I am sure you must be in a hurry to get to Aruba for your date."

I looked down at the floor. "Mia, you know I don't have a date."

"I didn't know that, Bob, but I had strongly suspected that was the case."

"I didn't lie, and I did not say I had a date, I said there was someone I wanted to see there. That makes a difference."

"Am I allowed to ask who it is that you wanted to see?"

"It was the doctor that took care of me after my accident. He asked me about the accident, and I told him I would tell him about it sometime. I was just going to do that."

"All right, I will forgive you. Does that mean we have a date for tonight?"

"I will beg if I must."

"That won't be necessary."

Mia and I had a lovely date that night. I think it brought us closer together. The thought that I may lose her made me like her even more, if that is even possible.

The weekend did reach some form of normalcy. I spend a lot of time with my pilots. I wanted to get to know them better. I tried to get inside their minds and learn everything about them I could.

I talked to Mia while we were at dinner and told her I would like to have my pilots meet some nice ladies. I told her that all were gentlemen and possessed high morals. I would not hesitate to introduce them to anyone.

Mia seemed to be pondering that question for a short time. Finally, she offered. "Bob, I think it would be appropriate for us to have a gathering, or dinner, to introduce them to the citizens of Rutling. Rather, perhaps it should be an introduction to yours and my friends. That would include many of my lady friends."

"That sounds like a terrific idea. Where would you have it?"

"Since it is not an official state function, I think we should use somewhere like the restaurant we are familiar with. I know they have a banquet room that we could use. I am a member of a large book club, which is composed of a lot of ladies that I can invite. Perhaps I should just invite them. There are a lot of single girls in the club. I know they would all enjoy meeting your pilots."

"Mia, that is an excellent idea."

"I will get started on it. I think next Saturday would be a perfect time. We have a meeting scheduled for then, so they should all be planning on attending."

"Mia, you are absolutely fabulous. Do you mind if I like you just a little bit more?"

"I think I can allow that if you will allow me to do the same."

"I think you know the answer to that."

The start of the next week was rather uneventful. We continued to monitor the radar and intercept anything that looked even remotely suspicious. Such sightings usually turned out to be private or chartered planes. We did sweep the coast often but stayed out of airspace owned by other countries. I learned that some of our agents had infiltrated Zebra's ranks and were supplying some useful information. It did indicate that they were doing very little flying. They wanted to keep a low profile, we were sure.

Mia had done a super job organizing an introductive party for her book club and my pilots. I had told my pilots that attendance was mandatory and suggested they wear a suit and tie.

The party was a huge success. The ladies were sufficiently impressed, and my pilots were perfect and charming gentlemen.

After the meeting, we adjourned to an outside café that possessed a mystic atmosphere. Not to mention a very romantic and picturesque view of the beach and ocean. Those that had stayed settled in to enjoy that view while those who decided to enjoy an exotic cocktail did so. I ordered appetizers for all and invited all who cared to have dinner with Mia and me, when they were ready, to order what they would like for dinner, it would be added to my bill as would the cocktails.

Some of us decided to take a romantic walk on the beach and watch as a fire-red sun slowly touched the ocean and sank into its depths.

As Mia and I walked on the beach, the sun, in its fading light, seemed to silhouette Mia and adorned her with a gown of red and gold. She seemed to wear a crown that was shooting fire arrows into the heavens.

I had to stop and look at her. "Mia, I thought before you were a goddess. Now I know. You take my breath away and fill me with hopes and dreams. Hopes and dreams that I can't reach out and touch."

"Why can't you touch those dreams, Bob?"

"I have an uncertain future that could destroy those dreams. The dreams would then destroy me."

"Bob, dreams are really wishes your heart makes. What do you wish for?"

"I wish I could tell you how much I like you, but I am not allowed to. I have not been given permission."

"Whose permission do you need?"

"Yours, Mia. Maybe I could have permission to say I like you just a little more than I did yesterday."

"I think I can allow that. That can be a good starting place."

"Mia, I am starting to like you a lot, but I am not sure how long I can keep it just there."

"I am starting to like you a lot too, Bob. It is a good place to be right now."

I moved closer to Mia, kissed her, and held her ever so tight. "I like you a lot now, Mia."

"I like you a lot now too, Bob." As she kissed me again, I felt something within me that I have never felt before.

CHAPTER XII

On Monday morning, as I walked into our squadron area, I was handed a dispatch from Admiral Dean that said he would call me on an encrypted line at 1000 hours today and be standing by for it. I went to my office and waited, wondering what it was all about.

At precisely 1000 hours, the call came in. I answered it with, "Hello, Sir; this is Lieutenant Commander Baker. "Hello, Bob. This is Admiral Dean."

"Yes, Sir, what Can I do for you."

"One of our operatives reported that Zebra would be moving an important cargo to an island off Haiti or possibly another undisclosed destination. We think this will happen Thursday, early morning. We are not sure if it is the plans or a substance for a very powerful bomb. We want this intercepted and destroyed. We would like to have it, but I don't think there is a way to capture it."

"It will be your job to intercept the plane it will be on and destroy it. We want you to get your planes ready and stand by them as soon as possible. You are not to leave your airfield and stay in readiness from now on. If we do not get a report, and the plane is in the air, we will expect you to have your radar active and detect it."

"Sir, I will be waiting for your call. We will maintain a full alert."

The Admiral said goodbye and hung up.

All my pilots were in the ready room, as I had directed. I hurried to the ready room to talk to them.

I walked into the room. "Everyone listen up. As of now, no one is allowed to leave our squadron area without my permission. We will be on full alert and ready to man our planes immediately. That means you are to be in flight gear and prepared to fly. I want you in the air in record time. Mike, you are in charge of the ground personnel. You are to have ground crew standing by the airplane. I want the planes pre-flighted and running by the time you get to them. We will make section take-offs in pairs to save time joining up. We will operate in pairs unless you can join up after we are in the air. This will be a twenty-four-hour alert. Get your gear together, and remain alert at all times. Any questions?" I was greeted with silence.

I wanted to inform President Villa about the current situation, but not leave our squadron area, so I called him and asked if he could come down or send someone down. I did not want to use the phone, but I had to keep him informed.

It was only a short time before President Villa walked into my office. "Bob, you sounded very serious, what is happening."

"Sir, we have something going down that you need to be informed of."

"What is it, Bob?"

I explained the situation and told him I would notify him, day, or night, what was going on. I told him I had devised a simple way for us pilots to communicate while we were in the air. I was sure the opposition would be tuned in to our frequency to monitor us. After takeoff, we would switch to radio channel six. When I said bingo, we would go up two channels to channel eight. When I said bingo again, we would go back three channels, or channel five. We would follow this pattern to confuse those who I knew will be listening. If we become confused, I would go to the guard channel and just say a number like six. That would be a signal for everyone to switch to channel six and start the sequence again. It is imperative that the enemy does not know where we are or what we are doing. I continued. "Sir, if you need to break in, do so, but do not identify yourself. If I need to know it is you, I will ask in a way not to alert the opposition. I will just say the word 'jackpot.' You can return with the word 'Reno,' and I will know it is you. Do you have any advice, Sir?"

"What do you think they have, Bob."

"I have no idea, Sir, but it must be worth eliminating."

We shook hands and bid each other goodbye.

I told Jim to make sure the planes were ready and fully armed. I wanted two extra planes ready. If one of the first planes would go down, we will have backups.

Now, all we had to do was play a waiting game. The waiting game continued through Wednesday. At about 0200 Thursday morning, I received a call from our operations. "The game has started." We had our signal that they had picked up some suspicious aircraft on the radar.

"We will be there. What time will it start?" I was asking them the bearing the target was on. "0200 hours, Sir."

"Thank you. We will be there."

My pilots were already getting ready, Jim said. "They are getting our planes ready, Sir." I grabbed my gear and started out the door behind the other pilots. All six planes were running and ready when we arrived at the line. We had a bright moon, which allowed us to move around easier.

Pat was right behind me as I started for the duty runway. He pulled up on my right wing when we taxied onto the duty runway. I gave him the signal to go to full power and held up my right hand. Pat gave me a thumbs up. I eased my throttle back a little so he could stay with me and dropped my hand, telling Pat to release his brakes and start our roll. We were in the air in seconds. I had the heading and altitude of the unidentified planes, so I set a course to intercept them. I knew they were about a hundred miles away. They were moving at a ninety-degree angle to us, so I calculated we would intercept them in about thirty minutes.

Jim and Mike had been able to catch and join up on us, so we continued as one unit.

I knew they were at 15,000 feet, so I went up to 16,000 feet to give us the advantage. The moon was offering a ghostly light, but it also gave us good vision. We should see them first because we knew about where they were. They did not even know we were in the air, so we had an advantage.

I knew I was getting close, so I keyed my mic and asked where the ball game was at. I just got back, "two-eight-five at fifteen." I knew that meant they were on a heading from us of two-eight-five degrees, and 15,000-foot altitude.

"How far is it to the ball game?" I asked.

"About fifty miles."

As I drew closer, I strained to see if anything was in front and below us. After a while, I was sure I saw running lights, but only one set. Surely, they would not have on running lights if they were trying to avoid detection. That is unless the fighters needed them to stay with the big plane. It could be a commercial plane. I was not able to detect any other lights, so I was not sure, and I needed to be sure.

"Bingo." That was the signal to switch channels to channel nine. Before the target planes could search for us and find us on the radio, I added. "I need input from the big dogs." I wanted instructions from someone with higher authority.

Suddenly, I didn't need it. I saw tracer bullets coming toward us from the larger plane and dropping off short. Someone had panicked and fired too soon. We were out of range, so the rounds were dropping off short.

"Bingo," I yelled into the mike. I allowed a few seconds for everyone to switch to channel seven. "Jim, look for the escorts, I'll take the big guy." Jim broke up in a climbing arc in case he had anyone behind him. I knew he would continue the ark back down in case someone was trying to get a shot at him. They would have to obtain a lead on him to bring their guns to bear. He knows if he

167

could stay in a tight turn, he could prevent that. That would give him time to look for them.

It was starting to get a little lighter. At this altitude, we would see the sun before the rest of the world did. I knew I was out of range of the large plane's guns, but I was not sure what might be behind me, so I too pulled up into an arcing turn, only I went to the left. "Pat, get my back." Pat broke off and made a sharp turn to the left. I knew Pat was after someone following us. He might have to take a head-on shot, a maneuver that took more guts than anyone can ever imagine. He gained all my respect at that moment.

I continued my ark to the left and started down. I was above the plane and making an almost vertical dive. I knew they would have a difficult time bringing any guns to bear on me. Out of the corner of my eye, I could see a burning plane. I shuttered, thinking it could be one of us. I would only have a couple of seconds to fire at the speed I was going. I would pass close by them, which would allow them to get a shot at me, but I was going so fast it would be an almost impossible shot.

I held my trigger down for as long as possible and missed a collision with their wing by only a few feet as I passed by them in a near-vertical dive. I heard what sounded like a woodpecker. I knew I had been hit. I wasn't able to see how bad I had hit them until I started climbing back up for another pass. I climbed to about five hundred feet above them in preparation for another run. Suddenly I saw a small fire in the left engine of the plane below me and watched as four parachutes blossomed in the air below the plane. I watch as the plane was slowly being consumed by the flames. The left wing broke off at the engine. The aircraft drifted off into a spin and fell toward the ocean in a fiery mass.

I was jolted back to reality as something hit my plane. Something exploded at the tip of my left wing. I watched as about a foot of the wing disappeared. I knew my controls had suffered some damage, but I still had most of the control over my plane.

I sat here in a daze as I watched an ME-109 pull up on my left wing. The pilot signaled me to switch my radio to channel two.

"May I have the pleasure of knowing who I am flying with?"

I thought I recognized the voice. "Otto, if that is you, it wasn't very nice of you."

"I thought that could be you, Bob. I had hoped it would be. It wasn't like you to go to sleep in combat."

"I think I am getting tired of fighting. I am glad it was you. I couldn't stand it if some amateur shot me down."

"I think I just evened the score. We are even now. I hope you don't want to go for the best out of three times. Do you, Bob?"

"I would prefer not to, Otto. Why don't you come over to my place for a drink? I know a nice little place that we can go to and roll dice for the championship."

"I would like to, Bob, but I don't think I would like the welcoming committee. Do you think you can make it back?"

I'm not sure. You did a pretty good job on my plane."

"Bob, why don't I walk you home. Can you call your guard dogs off?"

"Let me call them, Otto. I am going to guard to see how they are and get them on our channel."

"Go ahead, Bob, I can wait."

I switched to the guard channel so I would broadcast on all the channels. "This is Bob. Everyone check in on channel two." I switched to two and waited. "Bob, this is Jim. I have Mike with me. He is a little shot up, so I need to get him back to the base."

This was followed by. "This is Pat. I'm all right. What do you want me to do?"

"Everyone, go back home. I have a friend that will see me back." All acknowledged.

Rutling tower came up on the radio and wanted to know what happened. The President had been listening.

"Tell the President that everything is all right, and I will fill him in later.

"Otto, are you still on the horn?"

"I am, Bob. I am running a little low on fuel. I can get you most of the way home, but then I will have to leave."

"I would appreciate your company, Otto.

"Bob, I would like to see you again. Do you think we can work that out?"

"I know we can, Otto. Why don't we plan another meeting as we did before? We can meet and decide where to go."

"I think that will work for me, Bob. When do you want to set it up?"

"I would like to have time to talk to some people here, so I would like a little time. How about a week from today at 1000 hours?

"That will work for me. I think it is time for me to go home. Will you be all right now?"

"Everything is running good, just may have to land at a higher speed to compensate for my damaged wing."

"Sorry about that, Bob. If I had known it was you, I wouldn't have done that."

"I know that, Otto. You and I can change the future. We can't change the past. Let's look ahead, not back. I will see you in one week."

"I'm looking forward to it." Otto gave me a salute, which I returned, and broke away.

When I landed at Rutling, I was told to contact the President as soon as I could. As soon as I landed, I got to a phone and called President Villa.

"Bob, can you come over? Admiral Dean wants an update and wants to talk to both of us."

"I will be there in a few minutes, Sir."

When I arrived to see the President, Mia was waiting outside the President's door. She just threw her arms around me and said. "Bob, I was so worried about you."

"I was sure you would be. I'm back now. We will talk later. I need to see your father now."

I knocked on the President's door and was told to come in. President Villa was standing there with an outstretched hand for me to shake. "Come in, Bob. You gave us all a scare. Admiral Dean wants an update. He will be calling soon on a secure line." President Villa had hardly finished talking when the phone rang. The President picked it up and said, "Hello." There was a short hesitation after which he handed me the phone. He didn't need to say anything.

I just said, "This is Lieutenant Commander Baker."

"Bob, this is Admiral Dean. Sounds as though you had an eventful morning."

"Yes, Sir, I did. I will fill you in on what happened. We intercepted a twin-engine plane escorted by four 109s. I shot down the twin-engine. It appeared that there were four men in the twin-engine plane I shot down. I believe all four made it out all right and landed on or near a small island. The plane crashed into the ocean and, I am confident, was destroyed along with whatever was in it. I believe all four occupants that were in the plane and bailed out are on or near a nearby island North of Aruba. I do not know their condition."

Admiral Dean replied, "I will dispatch a Catalina seaplane that will be there in a couple of hours. They will evaluate the situation and advise us of what that situation is. We also have ships in the vicinity that can be there in several hours. A submarine is thought to be very close and is also heading that way. They can land a detail very soon to detain the survivors until we can land more forces. What is your condition? Did you, or any one of your pilots get hurt?"

"Not that I am aware of, Sir. I think one may have taken some damage to his plane, and I did get shot up a bit, but I think everyone is all right."

"Did you receive any personal injuries, Bob?"

"No, Sir. I could have, but it was the German Major I think I have told you about that damaged my plane. He could have easily shot me down, but he did not. I have a meeting with him scheduled in one week. I need your permission to see if we can end hostilities. I believe that can be attained without much difficulty."

"After we have the current situation in hand and have more information, you and I will deal with that. I would like to have this settled peacefully."

We concluded the meeting and hung up.

When I left, Mia was not there, so I drove back to the squadron. I wanted to check on my pilots. I was concerned about their condition and needed to find out all that had taken place.

All my pilots were in the squadron area waiting for me. There was a lot of excitement. Jim had brought one of the ME-109s down. He had gotten on his tail and stuck with him, getting intermittent shots until he saw a lot of smoke come out of the engine. Jim said he held off and allowed the pilot to parachute out.

"I think that was a good idea to do that, Jim. I would like to end this without any bloodshed."

Pat offered, "I got some good hits on one of the other ones, but I couldn't bring him down."

"How did you do, Mike?" I asked.

"I tangled with a guy that was really good. Every time I thought I had him, he managed to turn it around. He put some rounds at an angle behind my cockpit. I felt something hit the back of my seat. I am sure it was the machine gun that hit me. If it had been his cannon, I think it would have come right through my backplate."

I just smiled and said, "Don't feel bad. I pulled the biggest mistake I have ever made in combat. I was watching the twin-engine breaking up and never saw the ME-109 when it came up behind me. I was lucky it was the Major I went to see in Aruba. He thought it was me and shot the end of my wing off. He could have gotten me if he had tried."

Jim asked. "Did you see what happened to the twin-engine after you hit it?"

"I saw four chutes come out of the plane. Right after that, the left wing folded at the motor and the plane went into a spin. I didn't see where it crashed. I had some company about that time."

Mike offered. "I can tell you one thing, those guys were good. I'm kind of hoping we don't have to tangle with them again."

I patted Mike on the shoulder. "I am going to work on that, Mike."

We decided the best way to relax was going to the little bar we frequented, and as a good excuse, to relieve the tension.

CHAPTER XIII

I don't think any of us were feeling good in the morning. I told my pilots to take the day off and do whatever they wanted.

Mike and Pat had gotten acquainted with a couple of the girls from the book club. They decided to see if they would like to spend some time at the beach and have dinner later. The word had gotten out about our adventure the day before, so they were enjoying a little notoriety and intended to capitalize on it.

I asked Jim what he was going to do. "I think I will just take it easy and catch up on some letters."

"Mia told me one of the girls from the book club was kind of interested in you."

"Really, which one?"

"The one with the red shoes. You should remember her. She laughed at all your jokes, even the bad ones."

"Bob, are you serious? She was beautiful. I didn't think she acted interested in me."

"Mia told me that she called her and mentioned that she wished you would ask her out."

"You pulling my leg?"

"Why don't you call her and see if she wants to go to dinner tonight. I was going to ask Mia if she wanted to have dinner with me. We can all go out together. I think that would be fun."

"I don't know how to get hold of her. I think her name was Ruth."

"I intend to call Mia and ask her out. I am sure Mia will have her number. I can ask her."

"Bob, if you aren't pulling my leg, I would like to do that."

"I'll call Mia right now and see if she would like to have dinner this evening." I walked over to the phone and called Mia. She said she would love to go out and gave me Ruth's phone number.

Jim called and found Ruth was thrilled that he had called and would love to have dinner with him. I don't believe I have ever seen that big of a smile on Jim before.

The next morning, President Villa called and asked me to see him. He had a lot more news about what happened after all our previous activity a couple of days before. I told him I would be right down.

When I entered his office, he told me to have a seat. "Bob, we hit the jackpot. The island the men that bailed out were on was a rather small island with just a few people on it. When they saw what they were up against, they did not resist. They did have some small weapons, but they knew what would happen if they tried to use them, so they did not put up any resistance. Here comes the good part. Three of the four were war criminals. The other was just their pilot. The war criminals were very tight mouthed about what they were doing. The pilot decided to cooperate when he was told he would be charged with war crimes if he did not. It was suspected that they had to be up to something, and it proved to be right. You following me so far?"

"I'm with you, Sir."

"The pilot told us that they had gold and other valuables on the plane. They were moving them to another location because they would no longer be safe where they were."

"Sir, I thought the plane went into the water. If it did, the cargo would surely be lost. The plane was on fire and breaking up the last I saw it."

"It did go into the water, Bob. The water is not very deep where it went in, so we do have a good chance of locating it."

"The way the plane was breaking up, Sir, it could have scattered the cargo over a mile or more."

"We have one thing in our favor, Bob. We are quite certain that the valuables were in two safes. That means the contents should have stayed together. An effort will be made to find them."

"Won't an attempt be made to locate the rightful owner and return it to them, Sir?"

"Absolutely, and we do hope they will be found. It will be challenging, with all the items that were confiscated by the Germans."

"It would be nice, Sir, if the rightful owners were found."

"In any case, Bob. Whether they find the owners or not, there should be some sort of a finder's fee. If there is, it will probably not amount to a vast fortune. Whatever it is, it should go to you and your pilots. You are the ones who risked your lives to bring the war criminals to justice. I think it is reasonable to assume this could happen."

"I know my men would appreciate it, Sir."

"Bob, I am mostly thankful that these men have been captured, and I do hope our lives will change for the better. We do still have a serious problem, and that is the rest of the men from Zebra are still in question. We do not feel they are war criminals, but they did demonstrate hostile action against Rutling. They may be good men, but they are still criminals in our minds. They must be dealt with, Bob. I know you have formed a friendship with one of them. He has tried to put a stop to all this, but I am not sure that will weigh in his favor."

"Sir, you know I am to meet him in a few days. I had hoped they could be bargained with to disband now that the leaders have been captured."

"Do you really think they will surrender if they know they will face charges, Bob?"

"Probably not, Sir. Maybe they will just try to be absorbed into the population and assume other names."

"That is a very strong possibility. Do you think your government will accept that and let them go free?"

"I don't think they will pursue them. It is just too difficult, and they are not that important. What do you think the Venezuela government will do?."

"They will no doubt do as they have in the past, Bob. That is to ignore them and just turn the other way. The question is not what Venezuela will do; it is what your government will do. Maybe more of what they can do."

"I think you are right, Sir. There is not a lot they can do. I would still like to meet with Major Schultz. I think he is an honorable man. I am convinced he wanted to stop what was going on. I would like to see him vindicated."

"Bob, talk to Admiral Dean. If he leaves it up to me, I am open to that happening. Do you think you could get him to come to Rutling? Talk to Admiral Dean first and let me know what the situation is."

"I will do that, Sir.

Before I left President Villa's office, a dispatch came in saying that Admiral Dean would call here on a secure line at 1300 hours today. He wanted both President Villa and myself to be available. It was already 1100, so I decided to see if Mia was available. We could have lunch and spend a little time together. I did find her in another office working.

"Mia, I didn't know where you were, but I found you. Your father and I have a phone meeting at 1300, thought you might have lunch with me. I have missed not seeing you lately."

You have been very busy. I am about sick from worrying about you. I wish you would consider some other line of work. I would very much like to have lunch with you."

"I know what you are going through, and I don't like it either. Very soon, you and I must sit down and have a heart to heart talk. I am growing tired of what I am doing and would like to make some changes."

"I hope those changes are what I am hoping for, Bob."

"Any changes will have to consider you, Mia."

Mia and I had lunch and a pleasant visit. I was now sure I wanted to make changes, and those changes had to include Mia.

I was in President Villa's office before 1300 and ready to talk to Admiral Dean. We received a call and heard. "Admiral Dean would like to speak to President Villa and Lieutenant Commander Baker; are they available?"

President Villa answered, "We are both present and on a speakerphone."

The next person we heard was Admiral Dean. "President Villa and Commander Baker, I want to bring you up to date on what happened and determine our next step."

"We do have in custody, the war criminals we were after. A positive identification has been made. I am sure they will go to trial. We have located their plane and will attempt to recover it. I will keep you up to date on that. We still must deal with Zebra. It will be hard for us to pin anything on them except being terrorists, and that did not affect the US. Our hands are tied. We cannot go into Venezuela without their permission, and we all know we would probably never have that permission. I don't want to be blunt, but it is really up to you, President Villa, about what happens. I think you are the same as we are in that you cannot just go into Venezuela without a backlash from that country."

I broke in, "Admiral, are you saying that you will not go after the rest of Zebra and leave it to President Villa."

"In a nutshell, that is exactly what I am saying."

"Admiral, I have Met Major Schultz, who is in that group. He is an honorable man; in fact, he could have killed me a couple of days ago but did not. I am to meet with him in a few days to talk about all that has taken place recently and try to work something out. Do I have permission to take orders from President Villa and work something out to his satisfaction?"

"You are still a US military officer. I will allow this on a minimal scale. You will be acting for President Villa and not the US. If that is understood, I will allow this."

"Thank you, Admiral, I am fully aware of what you are saying."

President Villa interrupted. "Admiral Dean, I would like to keep Commander Baker here until we get this settled. It could take a while. We do need him."

"Mr. President, that will not be a problem. Bob, you keep in touch with me and keep me informed of what is going on."

"I will do that, Sir."

The conversation was ended.

President Villa turned and looked at me. "Bob, we need to go over a lot of things. I think I want to meet this Major Schultz. Do you think you can arrange that?"

"He is very wary. I am not sure, but I do think I can convince him to come here and talk to us. If you state the conditions under which we will meet, I will try to get him to agree. I am going to meet him very soon, so give me what you want of him, and I will try to convince him."

"Come over to my office tomorrow when you have time, and we will get some provisions for both sides."

"I will do that, Sir. I have a good feeling about all this."

"I also do, Bob."

I left the President's office and walked down to where I thought Mia would be. "Mia, I have some good news for you. At least I hope you consider it good news."

"What is it, Bob?"

"We just talked to Admiral Dean. It sounds as though he may let me stay here longer. I hope that is good news for you."

"Bob, that is wonderful news." Mia came over and put her arms around my neck and hugged me. "I wish it was forever."

"Just don't get tired of me, Mia."

"That will never happen."

"Mia, are you busy tonight? I would just like to have dinner somewhere where it is quiet. Somewhere where we can talk and dance. Just the two of us."

"I would like that, Bob."

"Can I pick you up at seven?"

"Seven would be alright with me."

"We can go to our little restaurant, find a dark corner where no one will see us. I could hold your hand and tell you how much I like being with you."

"I hope it will be very dark, Bob."

"I just need enough light to see you, and only you. It could be bright sunshine, and I still think you would be the only one I would see. I hope I'm not frightening you, Mia."

Mia came close and gave me a gentle kiss. "Do I look like I am frightened?"

"No, but I think I might be after that kiss. I will see you at seven."

I went back to my quarters and just tried to relax. I think talking to Mia did make me feel better. I yearned for us to be closer, but I could not help but consider what may be in store for me. I was back in the Navy again and could make a career of it if I wanted to. I thought that was what I wanted, but now I am not so sure. If Mia were willing to leave her island and go with me, we would be separated for months while I was on sea duty. What I would be doing was also not the safest occupation I could have. I had lost too many friends, not to realize that. I knew I was falling in love with Mia. I did not know if it was fair of me to ask her to love me if we had so many disadvantages.

I decided to put that all behind me for the evening. I wanted to enjoy being with Mia and not worry about what might happen. Someday soon, I would have to face reality and deal with it. Maybe Mia doesn't like me enough to consider marriage. Perhaps I should just wait and see what happens.

I was there to pick Mia up promptly at seven. When she came to the door, I felt my knees grow weak. To just look at her made me melt. "Mia, you look amazing tonight."

"Thank you, Bob. You look very handsome yourself. I am starved, you better get me something to eat, or I may not be able to dance with you."

"By all means, I don't want you to collapse. I am looking forward to dancing." I gave her my arm, which she took, and walked with me to my car.

We enjoyed a pleasant conversation on the way to our destination. After arriving, we did find our little corner in a somewhat darkened part of the café. If there were other people in the restaurant, I didn't see them. After we placed our order, and our wine arrived, I couldn't help but reach over and take hold of Mia's hand. "Right now, I think I am one of the luckiest men on the face of the earth. I can't think of any other place I would rather be. Unless, of course, you were there."

"I know how you feel, Bob because I feel the same way, but I am afraid. Afraid you will leave me. Afraid you will leave, and I will never see you again. Afraid I will be alone. Please don't do that."

"I am also afraid, Mia. Afraid that I will lose you, that something will tear us apart. I don't want to lose you."

Mia had a tiny tear roll down her cheek. I reached over with my napkin and softly touched her cheek to dry the tear. "Now, I am not going to say anything more. People are starting to look at us. They must think I am being mean to you."

Mia looked at me and smiled, "I am alright now."

"Dance with me, Mia." I stood up, took Mia's hand as we stepped onto the dance floor. As I held her close, I whispered in her ear. "Tell me when I can like you a little more."

Mia whispered in my ear. "I will, Bob."

We had a wonderful evening. A magical evening that left me breathless. I hoped Mia was feeling that magic and felt the way I did. I also knew we shared the uncertainty of our future if I were to stay in the Navy.

After dinner, I drove Mia home and was invited in so we could spend a little more time together. I was offered another glass of wine, which I accepted. Mia sat down beside me on the sofa. "How long do you think Admiral Dean will let you stay, Bob?"

"He didn't specify any time. He kind of left it up to your father."

"I think I will have to talk to Dad, so he will need you here for a long time."

"That would be fine with me, Mia. I like it here, and I like you."

"When you leave here, what do you think you will do or where you will go?"

"I would assume I would receive orders to a fighter squadron. With my rank now of Lieutenant Commander, I should be the executive officer. It could be other assignments, but that is the most likely."

"Bob, I worry about you and your flying. I wish you had a normal job like other people. It is just so dangerous. Look at the close calls you have had here."

"I know, Mia. I don't know what else I would do. It's the only thing I know. I know what you are saying, and believe me, I have thought about it a lot. It is very difficult to ask a girl to live with something like that. It is also the time spent away when you have sea duty. I would be gone for about nine months at a time. How do you feel about that?"

"I think you know without asking."

"Does that mean I am out of the running? Just when I wanted to tell you, I liked you a little more. That's not fair. Now I have to start looking all over again."

"I guess you just have to decide what is most important to you."

"That's not a very hard question to answer, Mia. I know what is important and what I want. There has to be a light at the end of the tunnel also."

"I am not sure what you mean by that, Bob."

"It isn't always what you want. The means must justify the end."

"I'm still lost, Bob."

"It isn't always what you want. You have to pay the price to gain what you want. I guess what I am simply saying is that you can live on love for only so long. The bills have to be paid too, and to pay the bills you need to have an income. Believe me, Mia, I wish I could get into another line of work. Not just any work, but something lucrative and something I enjoy doing."

"I don't understand how you can enjoy risking your life. It has to be something else, Bob."

"At first, I did not consider that I was risking my life. I loved to fly, and I was good at it. Even when a friend was lost, we had a defense for it. It was simply not to talk about him. Treat it as though it never happened. That was very true and very real, Mia."

"That is difficult for me to understand, Bob."

"That was the only acceptable defense. If you dwelled on the loss of a friend and became fearful, you were very likely to be next." I hesitated, looked directly at Mia. "Mia, since I met you, I feel different and think differently. I am tired of combat. I am tired of all the killing." I have something now that I want more than I have ever wanted anything in my life."

"Mia looked at me with a puzzled look. "What is that, Bob?"

"You, Mia, it is you."

Mia stood silent for a moment, then threw her arms around my neck. I could feel the dampness of her tears as they touched my cheek. "Thank you, Bob. That is the nicest thing anyone has ever said to me."

"Mia, why is it that I always seem to make you cry?"

"They are happy tears, Bob. Is it all right if I go first and tell you that I like you more now? A lot more."

"Thank you, Mia. I like you more too. Let's work on the next step now."

It was getting late, so we made our way home. I spent a few more minutes with Mia, kissed her, and said good night.

CHAPTER XIV

After I was up and about, I called President Villa and ask if I could see him sometime today. He suggested that we meet at 1300 hours. I told him I would be there.

I made my way over to our squadron and found all my pilots in the ready room. I was asked if I had anything for them to do, which I answered with a negative answer. I told them they could do whatever they wanted to do. We would not be in demand anytime soon. I did ask Mike to see that a plane was ready for me in the morning. I wanted it fully armed and ready. He asked me what I was going to do. "I guess I didn't tell you that I am going to meet Major Schultz tomorrow and see if we can settle any dispute we have."

Jim interrupted. "Do you need someone to go along with you, Bob?"

"Hopefully, it will be a friendly meeting, Jim. I shouldn't need any backup." I hesitated. "On second thought, maybe it would be wise for you all to be in the air. Last time the Major had someone follow him. That's when a bomb was placed in my plane and almost killed me. We will meet here at 1100 tomorrow. Make sure your planes are fully armed also. I will go over what I want you to do tomorrow morning." Everyone acknowledged me as I walked away.

I was back at President Villa's office at 1300 and knocked on the door.

"Come in, Bob."

I bid the President a good afternoon, which he returned. I was told to have a seat. President Villa began. "Bring me up to date about Major Schultz."

"Yes, Sir. I think you know the basics on Major Schultz. He has been friendly to me ever since. I first met him at our meeting with the Zebra leaders. The last time he could have easily shot me down when I spaced out after shooting the twin-engine plane down. I don't know why he threw in with the war criminals. I don't think it was for money, or that he was trying to get away from something. Perhaps he just wanted to get away from where the war had taken place. Maybe he just wanted to keep flying. I don't think he is a killer. Perhaps he just likes to fly. I will make it a point to ask him when I see him."

I think he has had second thoughts about being with the group he is in. I don't believe the Zebra group will bother us again since they have lost their leaders. However, we can't be sure. The best way is to break them up somehow and destroy their airplanes. However, that may not be easy to do. They may still have some of the treasure, but I don't think they do. There are a lot of questions that need to be answered. We will know a lot more if Major Schultz will talk to us. I will try to get him to come to Rutling and speak to you unless you just want me to find out what is going on."

"Bob, I think you are capable of knowing what to do. I will leave it up to you to make the right decision. Whatever you do, I will back it up."

"I appreciate your confidence in me, Sir. I will try to make the right decision. I bid the president good afternoon and left.

On my way out, I did see Mia. We talked for a short time and agreed to see each other tomorrow. I told her I had a lot I needed to get ready for and would be busy today. I had a funny feeling about all this. I don't know what it was, but I've had this feeling before when I knew I would be going into battle. Something wasn't right, but I didn't know what it was.

The next morning I was up early and went down to the squadron area to make sure everything was as it should be. Jim showed up shortly after I did. "You're up early, Jim. I didn't expect you to be here this early.

"I couldn't sleep, something is bothering me, Bob. I'm on edge for some reason. I had felt this way before a tough mission when I was in the Air Force. I don't know why I am on edge this morning. Just be careful today."

"Jim. I am going to meet Major Schultz near Aruba. Have your flight South and East of Aruba. Be at about 12,000 feet. I will meet the Major at about 10,000 feet."

"We will be there, Bob."

"Jim, make sure your planes are all armed. Test your guns after you are in the air."

"We will be ready, Bob.

I went out early to preflight my plane. While I was on the line, Pat and Mike showed up. Both walked over to me with Jim right behind them. Jim spoke up. "Bob, give us a signal if you think you are running into trouble."

Alright, Jim. I'll just say, the sun is bright today. That will be your signal to start over toward me. If I say, the moon is up. That will mean I may need your help. Get into an offensive position. If I say the sun has set, that will be telling you to take aggressive action."

"I've got it, Bob.

I finished pre-flighting my plane and climbed into it. As I taxied out to the duty runway, I saw Jim with the other two planes behind me. I received clearance for take-off. After I was in the air, I turned to the Northwest and started my climb. I heard Jim get clearance for take-off, so I knew he would be in the air and right behind me.

As I neared Aruba, I put out a call to see if Otto was anywhere near.

A call came right back. "Bob, this is Otto. I'm over a small island just south of Aruba at 10,000 feet. I'll set up a circular pattern around it. Join on me."

"Roger, Otto, I have you.

As I was coming in on Otto's wing, I caught a flash of light high and to the North. I looked up and saw a formation of planes about 2,000 feet above us.

"Otto, I think we have company high and to the North.

"I think that could be some of my friends, Bob."

"I thought you were coming alone on a nice day with the sun shining. That was my signal to Jim to start maneuvering for position.

"I would like you to come back to our base with me and thought you might like an escort."

"If the moon was shining, I may consider it." Again, that was my signal to Jim to get into position to attack if necessary.

"Bob, I am afraid you have no choice. You see, you have some friends of ours that we would like to have back. Just visit us until my friends are released. You can go home then.

"Otto, I thought you were a man of honor. I am very disappointed with you."

I watched as two ME-109s, one on one side of me, slip into formation with us. They moved in close so I could not break out of the formation.

'I'm sorry I had to do this, Bob. I have orders to get my friends back. As soon as they are released and back with us, you will be free to go."

"Why don't I believe you, Otto?"

"I give you my word."

"Right now, that's not worth much."

"I don't think you are in a position to refuse me."

I turned around enough to see three P-51s trailing us. I was sure they had not been noticed. "I think I am in an excellent position to refuse you, Otto. If you all behave and go home, we won't shoot you down. How is that for an offer?."

"I am afraid I will have to refuse your generous offer this time."

"One last chance, Otto."

"Sorry, guess you will just have to shoot us down."

"I would prefer not to do that. Look behind you, Otto."

A brief silence followed. "I see your point. I underestimated you, Bob. You're holding the winning hand. What next?"

"First of all, I feel that I should tell you that if anyone makes a sudden move, they will be shot down immediately. Now, I want you all to empty your guns. Fire in place until all your ammunition is expended."

Otto came up on the radio in German, I assume, telling his pilots to comply with my order. The air was rent with gunfire. I had pulled back with the rest of my pilots to be in a position to act if necessary. "Otto, the man on your right, did not empty his guns."

Otto, again came up in German. "Bob, he said they jammed."

"Otto, all guns do not jam at the same time. Tell him to try again, or I will give the order to shoot him down."

Otto again came up in German. The plane in question fired again. "Otto, I did not see any cannon fire from the same man. I am losing my patience with him. This is his last chance to comply."

Otto again came up in German, this time in a very agitated tone. This time the man in question complied.

"Otto, take up a heading of one-eight-five and start a slow let down to 5,000 feet. I did not get an answer, but Otto was complying.

I gave an order for each of my pilots to concentrate on one plane. I would take any stragglers if it were necessary. I told them they had orders to shoot them down if they did not comply and try to break away.

"What's going to happen, Bob?"

"We are going to Rutling. What happens is up to President Villa and Admiral Dean. I like you, Otto, despite what happened here today. I am sure you had a reason for doing what you did, and I want to know that reason. I pray that you are not guilty of war crimes. If you are all clean and can justify what happened here today, I will do all I can to help you, and that would include no charges and a release to go wherever you want."

"None of us are guilty of war crimes, Bob.

"In that case, I don't think you have a lot to worry about. I just don't understand why you did what you did today."

"I had to follow orders, Bob, and I was given orders to do this."

"That will take a lot of explaining, Otto."

We were getting close to Rutling. I could see it in the distance." Otto, Rutling is straight ahead of us, I want you to go into a regular break for landing. All your planes are to make a normal landing. Come to a full stop and cut your engines at the end of the runway. Take any personal weapons you have and throw them out on the runway where they can be seen. Everyone is to stay in their cockpit. Jim, Mike, and Pat keep an eye on the plane you have been following, don't land until all the 109s are on the ground, and the pilots are taken into custody. If anyone of them at any time tries to get away, you have permission to shoot them down. Did you hear that, Otto?"

"I did."

"Please make sure your pilots are aware and understand what I said." Otto complied in German to his pilots.

"Rutling tower, this is Commander Baker, did you follow our situation?"

"We did Commander and have people at the end of runway two-three to take custody."

"Otto, this is Bob, did you follow?"

"I did, Bob."

"Make sure your pilots know."

Otto, again came up in German.

"Otto, start your letdown and landing on runway two-three. Follow all instructions to the letter, so no one gets hurt."

Otto did not answer, but I knew he understood and would comply.

Otto took the planes into the break with everyone following instructions. As I came around to land, I could see that the pilots had been taken into custody. After we landed, I told my pilots that we would all meet at our ready room. Before we went to where they had taken the prisoners, I wanted us all to be on the same page.

When we did reach the building where the prisoners were. I saw President Villa right away. He motioned for me to come over to him. "Bob, how in the world did you get this done? I still don't believe it."

"I have some very good men working for me, Sir. Jim is the one that suggested that they follow me in case I would run into trouble. If Jim had not been on the ball, I wouldn't be here now. He is the one we need to thank."

"Would you excuse me, Sir? I would like to talk to Major Schultz. He did an about-face on our relationship. Maybe you would like to come along and see what he has to say."

"If you don't mind, I would like to hear what he does have to say."

"Pease come along, Sir. I think it could be interesting."

As we approached Major Schultz, he turned and looked at me and then dropped his gaze to the floor.

"Otto, what happened today? I thought we had established a good relationship. What happened to change it?"

"I was just following orders, Bob."

I stopped, realizing I had not introduced him to President Villa. "President Villa, this is Major Otto Schultz. Otto, this is President Villa." All I saw was a nod from each man.

"Otto, you're no longer in the German military, who are you taking orders from?"

"Bob, there are still active Nazis in Germany and here in South America. They have an invisible control. I still have family that would be in danger if I did not cooperate."

"I would like to know something, Otto."

Otto looked at me with a curious gaze. A gaze, or body language, that told me he wasn't sure what I was going to ask. I felt he might be hiding something. "I want to ask you again. Are you wanted for war crimes?"

"I am not, Bob. I was just one of the little pawns."

"What about the stolen goods? Did you receive any of that?"

"No, none of us did. We all knew about it, but I don't think they ever converted any of it into cash."

"Didn't you need to buy personal items?"

"The place we were at, in Venezuela, was owned by a very wealthy man who owned an exceptionally large amount of land. He provided everything we needed. We did not leave his property."

President Villa spoke up. "Otto, I hope you are being honest with us. We will check you out yet today. Bob, I will talk to you in the morning.

"Yes, Sir."

President Villa walked away.

Otto had a curious look when he asked me. "What happens now, Bob?"

"I am not entirely sure. I don't think Admiral Dean will get involved if you, or any of the other pilots, are not guilty of war crimes. We will have to tell him about the situation, but I think that is as far as it will go. I wished you didn't have to stay here locked up."

"I understand why, Bob. I am sorry I had to do what I did today. I was fearful for my family."

"I think I can understand that, Otto. Do you think your family will be safe now?"

"I think they will as long as I tried to do what they told me to do."

"What about the other pilots, Otto. Are you sure they are clean?"

"As far as I know, they are. I think you will find out if they are not."

"I'm sure we will, Otto."

"Bob, I think most of the others at our camp will leave. I think they know what could happen after today. They were all on edge before we left this morning. Now they will just want to get away in case the US comes after them."

"We will look into that possibility. I hope they do. It would make it easier to deal with. What kind of men are the ones that were with you today?"

"They are good men, Bob. I trust both of them."

"What will you do now, Otto."

"Bob, I wish I knew. I do not have any place to go unless I go back to Germany. I don't have a lot of money, not even enough to get back to Germany. There is not much left to go back home to anyway. I could go back to Venezuela, but I have no way of paying for anything."

"What did you do before the war?"

"All I have ever done is fly. I don't know how to do anything else."

"That is the same way with me, Otto. We have a lot in common. I don't think you have any plans tonight, so I will see that something proper is sent over for dinner for you and the other pilots. If you don't mind, I will join you and bring some wine. I would like to meet the other pilots."

"Bob! Thank you."

"You're quite welcome, Otto."

I wanted to see Mia, so I drove to where I knew she would be. I found her in a lounge reading. I stepped into the room and just said, "Mia." Mia dropped her book and rushed into my arms.

"I have been so worried about you, Bob. I have constantly been praying for you to return to me. I don't want you to ever be out of my sight again."

"I am sure those prayers are what brought me back to you. Mia. I want more than ever to change my life. I want you in it. I have set up a meeting with the German pilots this evening. I think I need to meet all of them. I am sure your father and I will need to spend time together tomorrow. When we finish, I want to spend the rest of the day with you. Can you arrange that?"

"You know I can."

Mia and I shared a passionate kiss before we parted.

After I arrived home, I called Jim and told him, if he and the other pilots wanted to meet our German counterparts, to be at where the prisoners were at 1830 hours. We would have dinner with them.

I then called a catering service and arranged an adequate amount of food and wine to be delivered at 1900 hours. I showered and made my way over to where the German pilots were.

All my pilots showed up. I had hoped and prayed that there would not be any animosity among us. My prayers were answered.

I couldn't help but wonder why we have wars. Why people want to kill each other. I now realize that we are only pawns. Pawns that are used by others because they are too fearful of doing it themselves.

The next morning, I called President Villa and asked when he would like me to meet with him. He told me to come down whenever it was convenient for me. I told him I would see him as soon as I could get there.

We did call Admiral Dean. We were told to handle it as we saw fit but to contact him if something significant came up.

CHAPTER XV

President Villa and I talked at length about what had happened and what we should do. We had received an answer to our inquiry about Major Schultz and the other pilots. There were not any records on the other two German pilots. Major Schultz had an impressive background and history. He had distinguished himself with his flying ability.

We decided to have the pilots choose what they wanted to do. We did put some restrictions on it, however. In anticipation of this, President Villa had sent for them, so they were in a nearby office. The two of us walked down to that office to talk to them.

The two German pilots that were with Otto had decided to go back to Venezuela to get their possessions and find a way back to Germany. Otto was undecided. We did learn that after the war criminals were apprehended, we had overestimated how many planes and pilots Zebra had. I had destroyed or severely damaged four 109s at our first meeting. Later, when we shot down the war criminals, we eliminated three more 109s. We had now just captured three more. We learned they only had fourteen 109s to start with, so that left only four in their possession. One of those had been severely damaged in a landing accident. They now only had three flyable planes.

Otto told us that the war criminals had taken all of the valuables with them in their plane. That was now in the ocean. He was sure now, with the failure of the last mission, the remaining people would disappear into South America or go home to Germany. Some of the pilots may have taken the planes, but he doubted it since they would be like a red flag wherever they went.

President Villa questioned him about any secret plans or material that may have been in their possession. He was sure there was none. At least none that he knew of.

I had to ask. "Otto, it will be difficult for the other pilots to get back to Germany now. The travel would be difficult, and everyone is short of money."

"Young men don't think of those things, Bob. They just find a way and do it."

"What about you, Otto. If you don't go home, what will you do?"

"Maybe I can find a job for a while. I would like to continue flying if I can. Germany will probably never be the same, so I don't think I want to go back there."

"What about your family in Germany?"

"My father is a doctor, so I think they will be alright."

President Villa spoke up. "Otto, none of you will be confined anymore. You and the other pilots can stay here on Rutling until you make the necessary arrangements to leave."

"Thank you, Sir. That is very generous of you."

President Villa stopped and thought for a minute. "Otto, we have a fund that I can draw from so you can get some of the things you need. I will assign someone to see that you can get around and get what you need."

Otto thanked President Villa again.

President Villa and I left and walked back to his office. Since we had concluded our business, I decided to find Mia and spend some time with her.

I found Mia working in a nearby office. "Good morning, Mia. I hope you're not too busy to spend some time with me today."

"I am never too busy for you, Bob. Did you and Dad get all your business finished?"

In a joking manner, I said. "I certainly hope so. I just told him I had a lot more important things to do than talk to him." Mia walked over to me and gave me a welcome kiss. "I hope you have reserved some time for me today, Mia."

"I have, just all day."

"That just might be enough. What would you like to do, anything special?"

"Yes, there is, Bob. I would like to talk some sense to you, and make you stop risking your life."

"I think that is pretty much over now."

"As long as you are doing what you are doing, it will never be over."

"Perhaps you are right, Mia. I have a suggestion."

"And what is your suggestion, Mr. Baker?"

"Wow, I didn't know we were going to get formal. Alright, Miss Villa, I suggest that you and I spend a casual day, like on the beach, and just enjoy each other's company. Later, we can have dinner and come back and talk. I mean a very serious talk. We have a lot of things we should talk about. I want to make some decisions, and I want them to include you. What do you say?"

"I say that I like your suggestion. I also want to say that I do want you to include me in your decisions."

"They are not just my decisions, Mia, they will be our decisions."

"Thank you, Bob. If we are going to the beach, I would like to put a swimsuit on."

"Me too. I will go home and change and come right back for you." I left and started for where I was staying.

Mia was waiting for me when I returned. I had brought some casual clothes along so I could change when we were ready to have dinner. We drove to a favorite spot on the beach and just enjoyed walking on the beach and sitting in our beach chairs, getting a little sun. It was a beautiful day. We were in a rather secluded area and very private. I thought maybe this was an excellent time to open up and talk.

"Mia, I think this is a lovely place and a good time for us to talk. Is that all right with you?"

"I think it would be fine, Bob. I am very anxious to learn what you have on your mind."

"You are on my mind, Mia. It is difficult for me to even think about anything else. You are all I can think about."

"Go on."

"I think I may have to leave here sooner than I expected. Everything is being settled faster than any of us thought it would. I think Admiral Dean will recall me when he notices we are getting things settled. I am still in the Navy, so I will have to do what he says."

"Where do you think he will send you?"

"I would guess, as I said before, it will probably be a fighter squadron, and that could be anywhere. It could also be some land facility, but wherever it is, it will not be here with you."

I looked at Mia. She had a frightened look on her face. "I don't want you to go, Bob." I noticed a tiny tear roll down her cheek.

"I don't want to go either. If I could find a way to stay, I would in an instant. Would you consider going with me, Mia?

"I don't think my parents would approve of me running away with you."

"I am not talking about you running away with me." I stopped for a short time and looked down at the sand. I looked up and directly into Mia's eyes. "Mia, I wanted to save this moment for a more romantic time. Also, a time when I thought your answer would be positive. I'm not very sure of that right now."

"Bob, you won't know unless you ask, no matter where we are."

"Mia, I have fallen helplessly in love with you. I don't want even to consider leaving here without you." Mia was still seated in her beach chair, so I slid out of my chair and onto my knees. I took hold of both her hands. "Mia, I can't leave here without you. I want you to be my wife. Will you at least say maybe or even that you will consider it?"

"Bob, I can't say maybe or that I will consider it, that would not be truthful." My heart sank. I was getting turned down. Mia continued, "I would rather say what I feel in my heart, and that is, yes, I will marry you. I don't have to think about it. You see, I love you too, Bob."

I think I went into some sort of shock. I couldn't speak, I couldn't even move for a few seconds. I had conditioned myself to hear Mia say no. I had conditioned myself to believe Mia would not leave Rutling. I finally gained my composure and let myself realize she had said yes. I know I was shaking when I took Mia in my arms and held her close.

"Mia, I promise you I will always be good to you and love you forever. I will spend the rest of my life making you happy."

"Bob, I promise you that I will love you forever too. I will do everything I can to make you happy and be the kind of wife you want me to be.

I kissed Mia and, once more, held her close to me. "If it will make you happy, I will try to find a different line of work. I will do whatever you ask."

"Bob, I want us to do what is best for both of us. We can make our decisions in life together. I think that is the way it is supposed to be."

"And that is the way it will be, Mia."

We walked hand in hand back to our car. I told Mia I had one more thing I had to do.

"What is that, Bob?"

"I need to get your parent's permission."

Mia smiled, "I don't think you will have a problem there."

We stopped long enough to get a sandwich and continued to talk to Mia's parents.

When I asked them if they would allow me to marry Mia, I received overwhelming approval. Her mother, of course, had to shed a few tears.

Mia and I talked on into the night before I went home. We promised to see each other in the morning.

The next morning, Mia and I met for coffee. I knew I would have to speak to President Villa about what I expected to happen, so I continued to his office after I left Mia.

I knocked on his office door and was told to come in. "Good morning, Sir. When you have time, I would like to speak to you about my assignment here with the US Navy."

"I have time right now, Bob. What's on your mind."

"I think my time here in Rutling is nearing an end. I am quite sure I will be reassigned quite soon. I think it would be wise to acknowledge that and be prepared."

"Have you and Mia made any plans for your future?"

"Not yet, Sir. We will do that very soon. If she wants, I will leave the Navy. If not, I would like to continue my career in the Navy. I am in an excellent position now and would like to take advantage of it. It will be largely up to Mia what I do. I want her happy above all."

"I am sure you will make the right choice, Bob."

We continued with my recommendations, which were to have Jim take over the small air defense we had set up until it was deemed not necessary. If that day came.

President Villa had talked to Otto and told me that Otto decided to go back to Germany. He thought he could offer a lot in the reconstruction of his country. I would talk to Otto before he departed.

I made contact with Admiral Dean and received a very welcome surprise. He needed a new aid since the one he had would leave the Navy now that the war was over. He offered me the position saying that he had been very impressed with the way I had conducted myself throughout my time in Rutling. He also complimented me on my combat record while in the fleet.

I was overwhelmed. I knew this would be perfect for Mia and myself. I also realized I would, with this assignment, be in line for a higher command position. I couldn't wait to tell Mia.

Admiral Dean would also give me sixty days to conclude my help with President Villa. It could not be more perfect.

I hurried to where I knew Mia was and found her in the office she frequented.

"Mia, I thought I would find you here. You haven't decided to back out on me, have you?"

"No, Bob, have you?"

"You're stuck with me. I won't let you change your mind. Have you thought about how you feel about being a Navy wife?"

"I know that is what you would like to do, Bob. Other women are Navy Wives and seem to like it or even love it. I am sure I can adjust to it and be happy."

"It is not what I want; it is what we want. That's the way this family will operate. I would like to add some excellent news I just received."

Mia looked rather serious and said. "What is that, Bob?"

"I just talked to Admiral Dean. He has given me sixty days to wrap up the loose ends here in Rutling."

"That's wonderful, Bob."

"Hold on, that is not all. He also offered me the position of being his aid. It would be some time before I would pull any sea duty, and it also means I would be groomed for higher command. This is something most men can only dream about. Give that some thought and tell me what you want me to do. I want this to be your decision too, Mia."

"I don't need time to think about it, Bob. If that is what you want, that is what I want too."

"Thank you, Mia. I guess this is why I fell in love with you. That and so many other reasons."

"Just think, Bob, we have sixty days to plan our wedding."

"After that, if we need more time, I can use some of my Navy leave."

And so it happened. Two lives became one. Dreams do come true if you follow your heart, believe in each other, and trust in God.

Made in the USA
Monee, IL
29 June 2020